To Ruth &

May this God
Inspired book open
your hearts to how
Much Family, Culture
& Love bond us together.
May You go with
God.

Love In
Christ
Mickey
Santure

# A BRIDGE THAT HUGGED Tomorrow

## A JOURNEY OF A SYRIAN WOMAN TO HER ROOTS AND A PROMISE

Dr. Minerva Santerre

WESTBOW
PRESS®
A DIVISION OF THOMAS NELSON
& ZONDERVAN

WestBow Press books may be ordered through booksellers or by contacting:

WestBow Press
A Division of Thomas Nelson & Zondervan
1663 Liberty Drive
Bloomington, IN 47403
www.westbowpress.com
1 (866) 928-1240

ISBN: 978-1-5127-3394-5 (sc)
ISBN: 978-1-5127-3395-2 (hc)
ISBN: 978-1-5127-3393-8 (e)

Library of Congress Control Number: 2016904054

Print information available on the last page.

WestBow Press rev. date: 3/30/2016

To my Savior, Jesus Christ. Without him, I am nothing. He has given me the ability to gain knowledge and to voice the love of my heritage through these words.

# ACKNOWLEDGMENTS

Thank you to my mom and dad, for without them, I would be nothing. They gave me the inspiration, love, and belief that I could do anything. I was their little girl. Because I was given the stars and beyond, I soared. Thank you, Mom and Dad.

Thank you to my soul mate, my friend, and my prince, Ken, who has stood beside me for thirty-nine years and has given me open-door encouragement to do and be anything in our marriage. He has stood beside me throughout the grueling nights of frustration while writing this book. Thank you, honey.

Thank you to my three grown sons, who have taught me the blessing of being a mother. It is an honor to call you my sons. I have the blessings of having two daughter in loves who have encouraged me and understood the legacy of family.

Thank you to my grandchildren, Bella, Jesse, Skyler, and Pearl, who gave me the insight to create a legacy of family long after I am gone.

Thank you to my family for the memories and love while growing up in a wonderful world of togetherness. I could not have written this book if not for you all.

Finally, thank you to my friends for always being there for me. You all encouraged me and trudged along with me. Life is definitely a bowl of bitter and sweet. You all help me weed out the bitter and embrace the sweetness of friendship.

*May this book encourage all who read it that with God ANYthing and ALL things are reachable!*

# NOBODY'S DAUGHTER ANYMORE

I watch as they lower the casket containing my mother into the ground, so beautiful, so sweet, such a peacemaker. People always called her "Mary the peacemaker." How much I will miss her! I pray that she somehow knows that I, her little girl, have always loved her, even when I was too busy being a wife, mother, teacher, and, finally, professor. There were always those tomorrows I had promised to put time aside to be with her and do the things that mothers and daughters do. But now? Now there are no more tomorrows. It is done. I put all the family and friends I have in this world before my mother, and I cannot replace that time. I am no longer a daughter to anyone.

Kevin escorts me to the limousine. I look up to the clouds and remember that my mother always loved bridges. She frequently told me that when my grandparents died, the bridge was broken. No more connection to the tomorrows. That is how life is with parents. The bridges that connect yesterday to today will end. The bridge of my parents is broken.

A memory sweeps over me as I recall my dad and mom holding my hands as we strolled through the promenades toward the Brooklyn Bridge. There we were, the three of us. How much love and security I felt in that moment. The memory sends chills down my spine. Why is it that when I think of the Brooklyn Bridge I think of terror?

I look out the window as we depart from the cemetery. It is a dreary, cloudy day. This weather takes me back to the time when my father—my hero—was coming home. It was 1963.

# My Hero

"Mommy, Mommy, what time is it?" I incessantly chanted.

Daddy was coming home from Korea. It had been three years since I had seen him. I remembered the day he left. It was Sunday, October 16, 1960, a cloudy, gray, dismal day. Daddy, Mommy, and I were silent as we made the trek from our brownstone apartment house in the Cobble Hill section of Brooklyn to Idlewild Airport. I knew that God must have been sad too because teardrops were falling from heaven.

The raindrops started flowing more rapidly in the last hour or so. I had been crying all morning. "Daddy, please don't go. I need you more."

Looking into my brown eyes, Daddy said, "Squirt, I have to go. You see, if I don't, someday the war against countries and mean people will be here, right here in America, maybe even in New York. I have to protect our country so that our country can protect little princes and princesses like you." He bent down and encompassed my little body with his big arms. "Now every night, Squirt, I want you to pray for your ole Sarge, and I will make sure to look at our special star every night at 8:00 p.m. This way, we can wish on the star together, and God will take our wishes and bring them to us. Before long, I will be back. Just keep that in your heart."

Daddy let go of me and went to Mom. He hugged her for so long that I thought she would stop breathing. Then he kissed her and let go. He picked up his duffle bag and started walking. He stopped and turned and said to me, "Every night, Squirt, wish upon that star."

Mom and I watched as his strong, broad six-foot frame became smaller and smaller until he was out of view.

My dad was the most handsome daddy in the whole world. I was such a lucky girl. He was my hero. He made me laugh all the time. He made living fun, and oh, how he loved to dance. I was missing the dancing already. Walking out of the airport, I thought, *Why are the raindrops as big as my tears? Is God crying a lot too?*

Now, three years later, Mom could barely keep me still. "He'll be coming back to me. Yes indeed. He'll be coming back to me. Yes, he is. He'll be coming back to me. He'll be coming back to me. He'll be coming back to me right today." I did a little twirl. "How do you like that song, Mommy?"

Mom was putting on her pearl earrings that Dad had brought her from his first tour of duty in Seoul, Korea. "My sweetness, that sounded like an angel singing. Now hurry. Go get your shoes on, or we will be late."

I wondered at that moment if I should ask Mommy if we could take my cousins, David, John, and Lizbeth, with us. They lived on the floor below us. I was an only child. I think God saw fit to put my cousins beneath me so I could have brothers and a sister. Then I thought, *No, this is really our threesome time together.* Not even Goldy the goldfish could come.

Mommy had made matching dresses for us. The top bodice was made of baby-pink chenille, and the waist bodice was gray kettle cloth with white stripes as straps that tied around our necks. Mom and I were the queen and the princess, especially today.

*Will Daddy look the same? Will he remember what I look like?* Mommy and I had sent him many pictures, but pictures become faded even in the pockets of the men who fight for our country. *When I grow up, I am going to talk to God about keeping the pictures clear*, I thought.

3

Mom and I slid into our blue four-door 1958 Pontiac, locked the doors, and began the arduous ride to the airport.

"Mom, do you think that Daddy will know who I am after this long? I mean, Mommy, do you think that he'll know that I have grown upped a little?"

"Yes, sweetheart. However, we still need to work on words. It is 'grown up,' not 'grown upped.'"

Mommy always had a thing for words. Whenever she wasn't busy cooking, cleaning, or working, she would work on crossword puzzles. Even though she did not finish high school, words and their meanings took her mentally to other worlds and countries and other periods of time. She always used to say, "Just close your eyes, and if you really concentrate, you can put yourself anywhere in the world that you like without ever leaving home." Reading was her favorite thing to do other than crossword puzzles—and being with me, of course. She should have been a teacher. That thought always ran through my mind.

"Now where were we?" Mommy said. "Make no doubt about it, you are Daddy's little girl, and he knows just how tall you were before he left. Now he will see how much you have grown! He will also see that you have become Mommy's little helper. I hope you know that I appreciate that too, honey."

Mommy's words warmed my heart to the core. I loved my mom.

I knew that Mommy could see me smiling from ear to ear. She wanted me to know that even though I was growing up, I would always be her little helper. I didn't want to distract her, so I turned away. If she could have seen my expression, she would have realized that I, too, wanted to be her helper, starting with loving her and Daddy.

The sun was shining so brightly that it made the hood of the Pontiac look like a shooting star; only the reflection really did not travel. I could hardly wait to see Daddy and what he had brought me. Daddy was always buying presents for us. We were

4

his girls, Mommy and I. Ever since I could remember Daddy always brought home gifts.

I looked over at Mommy. "Are we there yet?" Impatience was catching up with me. "Mommy, how long before we get to the airport?"

"Remember I told you that we have to look for Coney Island on the right side. Then from there it will be a hop, skip, and jump. Now try to think where we can take Daddy on his first day back." Mommy was always a step ahead of me in her thinking. I guess that was how it should be, and that is why mommies are so smart!

"Okay, Mommy," I said. As I turned to look out the window, I started to think, *Where would a hero like to go?*

Two blocks from our brownstone, on Court Street, was Louie's Pizzeria. It wasn't just any pizzeria. Louie's had tables with red-and-white checkerboard tablecloths. In the middle of the tables were beautiful red tapered candles placed inside wine bottles. At night, it looked so cozy—almost as cozy as the three bears' house had seemed to Goldilocks. Whenever I was there with my family, that's how I felt—as cozy as Goldilocks in the just-right bed. Or as my Grandma Hattie used to say, "As snug as a bug in a rug."

My mind drifted to Grandma Hattie, Dad's mom. She lived in the state that looked like a shoe boot, Louisiana. She lived in a little town called Bastrop, outside of Baton Rouge. When we used to go visit her, the smell of a paper mill was the signal that we were close. Too close to Mommy and Daddy. But I liked the smell. I wanted to bottle it up and take it home with me. Daddy would always say, "Squirt, you can't bottle up air." I would then argue with him and say, "Daddy, maybe I will invent something that can do that. Right, Daddy? I do have the smarts, don't I, Daddy?" He smiled. "Of course you do, Squirt. You're Daddy's little princess. So that makes you smart. Anyway, that's a dream, and there is nothing wrong with dreaming. Dreaming can turn into real life. You just have to believe."

I made my mind go back to where Mommy and I could take Daddy, our hero. I hadn't thought of but one place when I looked up and saw that we were at the airport. "Mommy, I thought of one place, maybe two. We can take Daddy to either Louie's restaurant or down by the water at Sheep's Head Bay. We can get the pickles and the rolls that Daddy likes. What do you think?"

Mommy smiled. "Those are two good choices, Michie. Maybe we can even take Daddy home and have a home-cooked meal. That would be a good choice." She winked her special wink that only she and I knew was one of a mommy and daughter's love.

"Glad that I was using my thinking." I could feel my smile turning into a half-moon shape. "What would we eat?"

"Well ..." Mom thought for a moment. "Remember Teta made grape leaves, coosa, kibbe, and rolled cabbage for Daddy for tomorrow?" She looked sternly at me, but her eyes were twinkling.

"Oh yeah! I 'member I helped!" I crossed my arms with pride.

"Remember is the word, Michie."

"Sorry, Mommy." I gave her my puppy-dog look.

She took hold of my hand. "It is okay, princess. It takes a lifetime of knowledge to know things."

I perked up and sat straight as an arrow. Mom smiled and said, "Well, if Daddy is not too excited about going out, we can take him home, put candles on the table, and have a special Syrian meal. Then we can go to Teta's and Jiddo's for coffee ... well, you can have milk and we can eat baklava. How does that sound? I think, Mommy, we will give Daddy all three choices. After all, he's our hero."

"You have that right, angel. Now here we are." Mommy parked the car in terminal J. That is where all the planes from the continent of Asia came in. We locked the car, and as Mommy took my hand, I realized that I was going to meet my hero, my dad, who I had shared with the whole country. He had protected everyone, especially the people in New York.

6

# HEROES ALL AROUND

The Three Mouseketeers. That's how I liked referring to us, John, David, and me. Well, there were really four, but Lizbeth didn't count. She was more like the queen mouse. She was bigger than us. Sometimes I really liked being with her, and sometimes I felt like she wasn't like us. Lizbeth was into dating and boys. Well, I liked boys, too, but not in the same way.

This day, John, David, and I were deciding what we were going to dress up as for Halloween. We weren't allowed to go past our block. In our minds, our block extended around the corner where our other cousins Jerry, Ritchie, and Geoffrey lived in a brownstone right next door to Vegetable Nona, Maryann's grandmother. Maryann was my best friend when I wasn't with my cousins. But then again, the only time I wasn't with my cousins was when I was in school. So I guess you could say Maryann was everyone's best friend.

Geoffrey was two years younger than me. He was closer to David's age, but because David lived with me in our brownstone, it felt like he was the same age as me. Oh, and John was two years older than me, but he was closer to me because he lived with David.

Halloween was just around the corner. Daddy had been home two years now and working at Fort Hamilton and also Fort Tilton. Everyday, he would come home with a new Golden Book. Well, maybe it was more like three times a week. Who kept track? Daddy was still my hero, and better yet, he was here. He and Uncle Paulie always made the days and nights fun.

John wanted to be GI Joe, of course, because he thought they had named GI Joe after his dreams to be a soldier or a sailor when he grew up. He wanted to save the world just like his daddy, my uncle Paulie. And just like my daddy, Uncle Paulie had served in the Korean War, but on a ship.

Uncle Paulie was my second hero. I loved watching him come home after work from the piers. He worked very hard. You also always knew when Uncle Paulie was around. The melodic though rough songs of Frank Sinatra came harmoniously through the brownstone. Between Uncle Paulie singing and Daddy dancing and playing the record player, we always thought we were in the presence of great stars! While Uncle Paulie sang, Daddy and I danced around, sometimes by the light of the big silvery moon.

But it was not always this peaceful for Uncle Paulie.

# THE SEAL OF FATE

The day was July 4,1942. Paul Semollini was ready for the navy. It had been his dream for as long as he could remember. He was going to be a topnotch sailor for the Unites States of America and protect the waters of the nation. He could not get over the battle at Pearl Harbor, which would be emblazoned in his heart and mind for the rest of his life.

He remembered that day well. December 7, 1941. He had just finished helping his younger brother with the paper route in the Red Hook part of Brooklyn when he walked in and yelled, "Il Ma sono a casa. Sono delle lì polpette di carne lasciate per il mio sandwich?" which meant, "Ma, I'm home. Are there meatballs left for my sandwich?" Mama would always respond, "Sempre affamato, il mio Paul. Il mio ragazzo. Sì sì nella cucina," which meant, "Always hungry, my Paul. My boy. Yes, yes, in the kitchen."

Angelina was sitting by the radio when it was announced that Pearl Harbor had been bombed. Countless sailors had been killed.

It was later reported that in total the navy and Marine Corps suffered a total of 2,896 casualties of which 2,117 were deaths (navy 2,008, marines 109) and 779 wounded (navy 710, marines 69). The army (as of midnight December 10) lost 228, killed or died of wounds, 113 seriously wounded, and 346 slightly wounded. In addition, at least 57 civilians were killed and nearly as many seriously injured.

The attack came at 7:55 a.m. Paul, as his friends and siblings called him, was just finishing a night shift at the Italian bakery that his uncle Diego owned. He was tired. When he walked in, he saw

Nuncio, his little brother, desperately trying to roll the newspapers that he had to deliver. He glanced at the clock: 7:55 a.m.

"Okay, fratellino, andiamo questa esposizione sulla strada. Ho una data pesante con un panino polpetta ed è solo 07:55 Per non dire che Salima dal basso angolo è in arrivo in giro oggi." ("Okay, little brother, let's get this show on the road. I have a heavy date with a meatball sandwich, and it is only 7:55 a.m. Not to mention that Salima from down the corner is coming around today.")

Salima was my mom's sister. Salima Zehabeen. *What a beautiful name!* Paul Semollini thought.

For the next six hours, he helped Nuncio deliver papers. Paul was not yet aware of the attack of Pearl Harbor until he walked in and heard the radio. "What happened?" Paul yelled. "Pearl Harbor was attacked today?"

So many dead! For what? For whom? For the freedom that surrounded the great United States. Right then and there, Paul Joseph Semollini was building his life bridge. He knew that he loved his Salima, but he also knew that was going to enlist in the navy and protect his country. Salima would wait for him. She loved him. But a question lingered for a moment in his mind: *Should I ask her to marry me? What if she says no? What if she says yes?*

These two thoughts disappeared as he cut his sandwich. "Ah Mamma, che lei è non solo la migliore madre nel mondo ma lei è il migliore cuoco nel mondo! Questo è perché non sono sposato ancora. Sebbene." ("Mama, you are not only the best mother in the world but you are the best cook in the world! This is why I am not married yet.") Paul smiled. "Although ..."

His mother looked at him. "Paulie, continuare prima che lei mi faccia arrossisce a molto. Andare vedere il suo inamorato." ("Go on before you make me blush too much. Go see your sweetheart.")

After eating his sandwich, Paul excused himself from his family. He ran the two blocks to Salima's brownstone and knocked on the door. Her brother Geoffrey answered. "Hey, Paulie, what brings you here? Oh, I forgot. My little sister. Sali Cue," he yelled. "Your Italian beau is here!" Geoffrey grinned as he let Paulie slip past the gargantuan front door.

As soon as Paul turned the corner, there was Salima. She was so beautiful. Her long black hair flowed gingerly to her waist. Her dress was made of silk with the design of moons embroidered all around the waist. He loved that dress.

*Moon over Salima. My own star that shines so brightly in my life*, he thought. *How can I tell her that I am joining the service? More Importantly, how can I not tell her? Today*, he thought as he walked over to her, *I will ask her to marry me.*

Salima walked over to him and kissed him sweetly on the cheek. "Let me get my sweater." When she came back, Paul grabbed her hand. Salima told Geoffrey that they would be back after a quick walk to the promenades and back.

As they walked along the promenades, Paul and Salima discussed the war, Pearl Harbor, and the turn of events for our nation. Nothing could be more important to a young man than protecting the land and soil upon which his feet rest. That was how most men felt. Salima agreed. Her two brothers, James and Tito, were in the army. She wanted them back so much, yet she knew the seriousness of war. She knew they had to do it.

Salima expressed this to Paul. Paul realized this was the time. Right in the middle of the promenade, Paul knelt. "Salima, I don't have much to offer you but myself. I do know that God brought you into my life for a reason. Salima, the reason," he pulled out a small velvet box, "he brought you to me was because he knew that you were to be my wife. Salima Antoinette Zahabeen, will you marry me?"

Salima opened the box. There before her eyes was the most beautiful, delicate engagement ring she had ever seen. "Paul Joseph Semollini, yes, yes, yes!" They embraced and kissed.

"Salima, there is only one thing."

Salima looked into his eyes and said, "Shh, I know, Paulie. It is okay. I will be waiting for you when you come home from the navy. I know where your heart lies. It is in helping our countrymen come home to the mothers, daughters, and sisters who are waiting." Out of their unending love for each other, tears of joy and happiness were bonded together.

The week went by in a flurry. Nona was busy crying and cooking. "Il Paulie, non la perdonerò mai se lei è doluto. Capire Mai! lei viene meglio a noi e ha a casa un matrimonio." ("Paulie, I will never forgive you if you get hurt. Understand, never! You better come home to us and have a wedding!")

"Mamma, come non può sono venuto a casa. Ho due belle signore che aspetta me. La moglie del presidente lei Mamma. Lei ha il mio cuore. La seconda signora, dolce, Salima che salima mia moglie. Sarà tutto la buona Mamma. Ora dove quel sandwich di polpetta di carne è?" ("Mama, how can I not come home? I have two beautiful ladies waiting for me. The first lady, you, Mama. You have my heart. The second lady, sweet Salima, who will be my wife. It will all be good, Mama. Now where is that meatball sandwich?")

That was how the two weeks went, in tears, plans for future, love abounding, and more tears. Then the day came when Uncle Paulie had to leave for basic training. Many new recruits were stationed far away from their families, neighborhoods, and young lives. However, Uncle Paulie was stationed not too far away. He was stationed at the US naval training camp in Boston, Massachusetts. Basic training was hard, but all the while, Uncle Paulie kept thinking, *This is for Salima and me.*

When Uncle Paulie finished basic training, he was given a two-week furlough before he pushed off on the SS *Blue Ridge*. There was a big party for him. Half the festivities involved, of course, Italian food and, of course, Syrian food. Grape leaves went well with meatballs. Everyone was there except the brothers who were overseas. The families danced and sang and ate until hearts and stomachs were full. There were tears of joy and happiness mixed with the sadness of knowing that Uncle Paulie was leaving for the South Pacific.

Then the day came. It was time to go. Uncle Paulie said his good-byes to all through tears and promises of returning. But to Salima he could not say good-bye. "Salima, let's just say we'll see each other by the sunrise and sunset of every day until my return. I will write you everyday on my lunch breaks, if we have one." He laughed, trying to make Salima feel better.

"Paulie, you know the rules. No looking at WAVEs, or any other woman, for that matter. Don't drink too much. Stay alert, and remember your prayers every night. Oh, and kiss my picture. I am waiting for you."

Salima could not bear to watch Uncle Paulie leave, so she turned and walked back to the car. The real reason was that she did not want Uncle Paulie to see the tears flowing like a river down her cheeks. She was never proud of crying, for she was a strong woman in those days.

Uncle Paulie knew that he was on a good ship. The Bethlehem Steel Company of Brooklyn, New York, had outfitted the ship as an amphibious force flagship and was commissioned on September 27, 1942. Commander Lewis R. McDowell, USN, was the commanding officer.

# A Heart Broken
# Wide Open

The weather brought a chill in the air. This time of year was not the prettiest in the northeast, particularly Brooklyn, New York. I allowed my mind to wander for a moment. The little girl had vanished. Was my imagination running wild, or was that little girl beckoning to me? Maybe it was because I had had no sleep the night before. In either case, I tried to quiet my thoughts as I turned to walk away from the sights and sounds of a city in pain.

More and more trouble had occurred since the February attack on the World Trade Center. I remember all too clearly that early afternoon. I had just finished my last course at the university. It was 12:18 p.m. The *New York Times* reported that a truck bomb was detonated below the North Tower of the World Trade Center in New York City. The 1,336 lb (606 kg) of a gas that is often used in explosives was in an amplified device that was intended to knock the North Tower (Tower One) into the South Tower (Tower Two), bringing both towers down and killing thousands of people.

Fortunately, the towers did not come down; however, the explosion did kill six people, and more than a thousand were injured. The attack was planned by a group of conspirators, including Ramzi Yousef, Mahmud Abouhalima, Mohammad Salameh, Nidal A. Ayyad, Abdul Rahman Yasin, and Ahmad Ajaj. Our country had been soiled by a group of terrorists from the Middle East that, although carried my culture, did not send the kindness that comes from the land of Jesus. Their hearts were evil. Eventually the four men were tried, convicted, and sentenced to life.

But now the fact remained that people around the world were seeing hatred in the eyes of a culture that I truly adored. How my heart wanted to shout to the world that not all of us were like the evil messengers! In every group there is bad. The shock wave began, only to give birth to an emptiness that somehow our freedom was being scorned by hatred. Hatred that my family had no part of.

My father and mother had taught me never to hate. That in itself brought a bitter taste to my mouth. How could people hate one another? God was watching out for us all, and hate was not part of the fruits of the spirit that aligned with being children of God. Looking back, I only knew love, hope, and peace—peace that my mother had shown me so many times. She knew that God wanted her to teach the fruit of the spirit that was taught to her so that I may have peace in my life as well.

I remembered the love my father taught me in an action that represented respect and equality. My thoughts drifted back to a time of my youth, when all I felt was encompassed by nothing but love. One day, Dad and I were walking on Fulton Street. It was a cold winter day, and dreariness had crept in. But that didn't stop the hero and his princess from going on a fun adventure. We were going to get hot chocolate at A and S's. It was really known as Abraham and Strauss, a department store on Fulton Street. but most people just called it A and S's. The thought of the savory hot liquid going down my cold throat made me walk faster. But not as fast as Dad.

We were about to cross the street when Dad saw a young lady who looked like she didn't have a dime to her name lying in the street. Others ignored her. How could anyone ignore another human being? Where was the love? The kindness of humanity? Dad showed me.

We turned and walked toward her. Dad extended his hand to her, took off his coat, and wrapped it around her. "You will be needing this," he said. We walked the woman, who had lost the hope of living, into A and S's. Dad found a security guard and explained the story to him. The guard, with his jolly Santa look, winked at me. "She will be okay. I will call the police and find her a new home by tonight."

Tears of joy fell down my face. I felt so bad for this woman. I didn't even know her name, but I didn't have to. She was a human being. She had a family somewhere who had brought her into this world. She was someone's friend. Now she would have us as friends. I couldn't bear to think of her lying there, cold and alone.

I am so glad that Dad didn't let the passing of time be swallowed up by the ignorance of people. He took the time to help someone in need. The clock of life ticked away but with beauty of humanity within my soul. Dad had shown me how to love and respect people, places, and things.

"Thank you, officer," Dad said.

"Squirt, I didn't think that I needed to buy a coat. I thought we were having hot chocolate. Oh, well. My coat was due for recycling, don't you agree?" We hugged each other and laughed.

"There's still time for hot chocolate, right, Dad?"

"You betcha," he said as we sauntered through the door of the restaurant after buying him a new coat. We didn't have that much money, but we had enough to share love and kindness to someone who did not. God always had a way of showing the good around me: The gift of love. The gift of my dad.

Then my mind came back to the present moment.

# SEEING THROUGH THE EYES OF A PROFESSOR

Kevin would soon be calling and wondering where I was. The meeting at the university had been cut short due to the weather forecast. This gave me a good reason to walk home from Saint John's University. After all, I reasoned, it was just three miles from the downtown Brooklyn campus to our studio apartment. If I walked the long route, it would have taken me right by my childhood neighborhood. Besides, I could have stood to lose a pound or two.

As I reached our apartment, the thought ran through my head again. Three years ago, the world stood still. New York wept, the nation wept, and all the people of the United States would never be the same. Yet there was a void in my thoughts.

September 11, 2001. I had just finished my doctorate in science education and was teaching at the school near the Twin Towers. Something in my memory could not let me see that time. This always happened. The minute that I let my thoughts run to that particular moment, my mind went blank. I remembered only bits and pieces of that moment. That it was a Tuesday. That it was September 11, 2001. What I wore, a purple dress suit. I had an important meeting at the university that evening, but it never took place. But the day had started normal enough.

My thoughts were interrupted with the ringing of my cell phone. "Hello? Hi, honey. I am running a little late."

"I was hoping that I would catch you. I thought you would be home hours ago."

"I know, Kevin. I stopped by the promenades."

"Michie ..."

"I know, I know. I just wanted to see how the point looked. Besides I had time to spare."

"*And,*" Kevin scoffed, "time to think, Michie."

"Yes, time to think. Now that I am not thinking anymore, what's going on?"

"Well, the hospital is having a meeting on the biochemical warfare and I thought I would sit in on it. As you remember, my favorite girl, I did my dissertation on that!

"How could I forget, Kevin? I was your personal editor." I chuckle. "Sorry, sweetheart. You are a genius in biochemistry but not in spelling."

"Okay, you win. What time will you get home, Michie?"

"I am on my long route home now, Kevin. I should be there by 8:00 p.m. Good enough?"

"Yeah, that will give me time to catch the meeting and be home for our evening dessert. What is it? Baklava?"

"Kevin, you I know I have to watch the waistline."

"But not tonight. Bye, bye, my wife."

*Kevin always has a way of making me smile,* I thought as I placed my cell phone back in my purse. He had grown accustomed to our food and our family. Food and family go hand in hand, especially in the auspices of a Middle Eastern family. The emotions churned in my heart, but it was more the culture that brought me to the overlap of thought. Culture sets the boundaries for the infant the moment he or she is born. Those boundaries are dutiful and respectful.

I gingerly rounded the corner of my street and thought, *Where did the humanity go? Is it all about who is on top of the world? Is that what we teach the children of tomorrow? How sad the world has become. It is a surreal world with no emotion. The emotion has been drained through hate, sterility to humankind, to intolerance to people who are different. When did the world get to be so mean? When did people think they could kill others just because they are different? Aren't all people born with a heart?* As I walked into our darkened apartment, I felt the quietness of the night and the cool air coming through the window that I had left open which ran a chill through me. *How can people be so hateful and spiteful? Haven't they learned that this world would be a better place if there were peace?* I looked at the street. It was so quiet, almost as if the world was asleep from fatigue.

So many lives had been taken. The terrorists completed an evil, evil task on September 11, one that will ring in the hearts of many for years to come. Yet not one culture or society has gone without hurting others. Why does the world blame Middle Eastern people? There is good and bad in all cultures. Yet the world still hates.

As I gazed at the streetlight again, I saw a little girl standing there. Who was she, and what made her expression so serene and yet beckoning me to go? And go where?

I checked the messages on the landline phone. The first call was from Kevin, reminding me that he would be late. I smiled. He ended his message with "I love you from the highest mountain. The love I have for you is higher than Mount Kilimanjaro. The sun rises and sets with you smile."

I then smiled wide, thinking, "That is my man. I know him in a way that no one else does. He reminds me always that I am still raising him." He has a heart of gold. The problem is he does not know how to show his love for me in public. When a mother has a child, she teaches that child to love. But with Kevin, he didn't have the opportunity for much love in his life.

# THE HEART AND SOUL
## OF SISU: BRAVERY
## AND RESILIENCE

In order to understand the culture of the one I love, you have to understand his or her culture and the heritage, lineage, and personalities of the parents who gave you the gift of your mate.

The boundaries were still evident in the philosophy of Kevin's take on life. He had wonderful parents. They lived in a small home in Renton, Washington. But to Kevin and his brother, it was a mansion and a dream of all little boys, for there was a park and baseball field right behind their home. Kevin's mother, Diane, worked the night shift at Boeing so she could be "Betty Crocker mom" during the day. At night she toiled with sweat and tiredness, but her heart was filled with the joy that morning would bring. Each paycheck she set aside money for the boys, "the nest egg for the children," she would say to her husband, Geoff. Diane took pride in what Geoff and she had. Coming from a staunch Finnish family in Minnesota had its benefits and definitely its boundaries.

The children helped with the chores before school. When afternoon came and the sun was almost setting, homework would be done. Dinner was placed on the table with no one asking, "What's for dinner?" but simply eating what was placed before them. "You take what you can eat and you eat what you take" was the motto of Diane's home growing up. While in her heart she wanted to set the same boundaries for her children, her desire was to present the boundaries that God desired for children. She was destined to be a Proverbs 31 woman.

# THE FARM

Diane's memories of the farm brought many happy times to mind. Yet the one that molded an indentation on her heart that lasted forever was the story of Martin, the oldest of her twelve siblings, and her with the daily chore of milking the cow.

Martin was the hardest to humor. He was also the hardest to understand. Some say that when he was a young boy, he was out in the sun too long, trying to ride a bull. The summers were known as Indian summers. Along with being extremely warm, the summers seemed short and the atmosphere was usually hazy or smoky with little or no wind. The story goes that Martin had had too much sun and it had affected his brain. But Diane never gave up. She kept her brother laughing when she would try to milk the cows.

As a young girl, she could never really aim the extracting milk into the bucket. Half the milk would land at her feet or on her dress, which was worse, as she had to do the chores before school. One day, Martin, in a staunch Finnish voice, said, "Little sister, ya have ta first love the cow and wish morning blessings on her before you try to gather the fruit of her."

Through tears, Diane said, "Love the cow? Momma will surely be upset with me for the mess that I have made."

Martin bent down, gave her a hug, and then extended his big burly hands and said, "Go on now. Cross the bridge, go to school, and learn for me. I will milk the cows in the mornings if you promise to come and give morning blessings."

Diane hugged her oldest brother with love that consumed her little body. From that day on, if anyone said anything bad about Martin, Diane was the first to stand up for him.

Every day, Martin watched Diane cross the bridge to a world he did not quite understand. The world of education was set to the side as his world was the farm and the family. Every afternoon, Martin would be there to see Diane running back from that world across the bridge to him to ask how his day went. The bridge always connected the two of them in a special way no one understood but God, Martin, and Diane.

Saturdays were special days. After the work on the farm was done, everyone came to sauna. It wasn't so much that there was a scarcity of water or places to bathe, but it was a ritual of bringing the family together. Female members would talk over coffee while the men would drink their beer or home-brewed white lightning. The children always enjoyed sauna because that meant all the cousins would gather on the farm. This tradition still holds true today. Saturday saunas were a bridge to the past and a connection for the family of the future.

Boundaries had their place in families, but bridges that stepped gently over boundaries were built. Bridges of love, Bridges of relationships, Bridges of life. Those bridges connected people to a lifetime of love, despite differences, even within the family.

# THE PURPLE
# STAIN OF LIFE

Geoff, Kevin's dad, came from a French Canadian family, whose family tree dates back to 1722, where Thomas Santrew came from Normandy, France. Descendants have noted that New France was established in 1660 and is what is known as the province of Quebec. The government of New France offered enticements to men from France to come to the province of Quebec that included land and money. From there, the Santrew family tree grew.

As the years and decades went by, some Santrews moved to Minnesota. This was where Geoff was raised as a little boy. The family background was that of magical hands that could do and accomplish almost anything. They were strong people, and as long as they had their hands and their minds, they would do anything that came before them, which included lumberjacking to now Geoff's profession, engineering.

Geoff spent his days as an engineer for Kenmore. His duties encompassed building the intricate mechanisms of engines for massive trucks put together by assembly lines. He did not take the knowledge he had lightly. His experience came from serving in World War II from his position on a tank. He not only learned to drive a tank but also to build or rebuild one if he had to.

As a young man, Geoff signed up for the army to protect what he believed in: the wind of freedom that feathered and gently swayed the Red, White, and Blue. He never forgot the sacrifice that so many of his fellow soldiers had laid down. Having come from a family of honor, he stood proud beside his fellow servicemen. He was reminded of that on a daily basis. When he was young, he wanted to help his country and to make his family proud.

But he and his father had boundaries that were hard to build bridges with and even harder to connect with bridges. The one thing Geoff knew would make his father happy was for him to sign up for the service. After all, his father had come home with a purple heart in World War I and his uncle was a colonel in the army. So on an October day in 1944, Geoff signed for the army. He was to report to Camp Roberts, which was near Paso Robles, California. He was to board a train from Seattle, Washington.

His stepmother, Bertha, packed him enough lunch for the trip. Geoff's natural mother, Olympia, had died when he was a baby. The story went through the years that she was standing by a closed window, watching a storm blow so strong that the house seemed that it would blow away. The windows shook from the incessant rain. She looked to see if the windows on the 1940 Plymouth were closed, gently opening the window and leaning out. At that moment, one that was forever emblazoned upon Geoff's father, a bolt of lightning hit Olympia and struck her dead instantly.

Geoffrey Sr. was not the same after her death. He tried to be a good dad to Dottie and Geoff, but it was hard. He was young and had to make a living to support the children. As the days wore on, it became harder for him to do a responsible day of manly work. He was an entrepreneur of sorts. Today, we call it a handyman. He took whatever job was available that did not interrupt bringing up the children. It was easy when Olympia was there, but now she wasn't and never would be again. Every day became more of a burden of will and thought. How could he bring up two children and still be the sole supporter for his meek family? His family lived in another state, and Olympia's family lived in Canada. Besides, Geoff Sr. really did not know them well. He had met her family just a couple of times. The times were scarce and so was money. The only time that Olympia's family came to America was for their wedding and for the birthing of Dottie and Geoff Jr. That was many memories ago.

There was no one to take care of the children except the young girl down the street. Bertha was fifteen years younger than George, yet she was mature enough to help with the children. She was seventeen years old when she started to watch Dottie and Geoff, and Geoff Sr. was thirty-two at the time. He was intrigued with her. Her smile was encouraging and forthright, and he began to see a future with her. Bertha oversaw Dottie and Geoff during the day, and Geoff Sr. paid her weekly wages to care for them. He thought to himself, *I am not getting younger, and Bertha would make a good mother to my children.* Needless to say, God was telling him that she would make a good wife.

Bertha and Geoff Sr. were married a year after they met, and she stepped into the soul and shoes as Dottie and Geoff Jr.'s stepmother. However, Geoff Jr. thought differently. He loved her. No, he adored her. When he looked up, he saw an angel looking back down at him. Dottie had recollection of their mother, Olympia, for she was only two years older than Geoff Jr. But he only remembered Bertha as his mother.

As the last moments came upon departure, Bertha was teary-eyed, and it took all that Geoff had in him not to start crying himself. His father, a man of great stature and staunch upbringing, simply said, "Make us proud, son. Be a man. You are doing it for our country." With that sentiment, Geoff said, "I will, Dad. I will."

Dottie gave him a ride to the station. Usually, they had much to talk about. On this day, however, the sadness of Geoff's leaving kept conversation to a minimum. As they approached the station, Dottie said, "You better come back in one piece, do you hear me? AND you better answer my letters! Otherwise I am just going to have to come get you and embarrass you. You know as sure as the sky is blue that I am good for that." She got out of the car and hugged her brother, sobbing, "I love you. You have and always will be my best friend. Not so good in the brother department at times."

Geoff looked down at her and with tears in his eyes said, "I love you, sis. Now don't go off and get married. You know I have to approve of the man who takes my best friend away from me. I will be back before you know it. Besides, courtship should take at least ten years, don't you agree?"

They both laughed and, with tearful eyes, turned away from each other. Reality was at hand. Geoff went to the ticket counter and Dottie to the car.

After basic training, which lasted eight long weeks, Geoff was sent to Fort Lewis, Texas, where he was processed for the trip overseas.

## Boundaries

Boundaries were ever present in Geoff's mind. Not getting close to the village people. Remembering the limitations of war. Instead of seeing women and children as human beings, he was trained to see them as the enemy. Bridges brought a vision of destruction rather than construction as yet another reminder of the war that had changed his life.

Geoff's mind always went back to the moment when his infantry was crossing Pusan in a jeep. His first thought was *What did I get myself into?* Sven, a big strapping Swede from Nebraska and Geoff's best friend, would always laugh and say, "It beats working in the factory."

On August 1, 1945, his infantry was ordered to drive on the road to Pusan. On August 3, 1945, a US general and other army officers gave the command to destroy two bridges as South Korean refugees streamed across, killing hundreds of civilians. One bridge ran across the Naktong River at Waegwan. As the sun shone on the bridge, Geoff could not help but see the girders that held the bridge. The hands that built the bridge must have spent countless hours bleeding as they toiled to connect the two cities that were lost in the sea of the purple stain of life.

Earlier that day, twenty-five miles downriver at Tuksong-dong, seven thousand pounds of explosives blew up a steel-girder bridge crowded with women, children, old men, and ox carts filled with their belongings. Many also drowned trying to swim to shore. Commanders were enthusiastic about this operation. The Fourteenth Engineer's report noted, "Results, excellent."

However, the news was grim for Geoff's infantry. Sven and Geoff were side by side in the artillery. Right before the bomb went off, Geoff turned to Sven, only to see his head blown off, leaving Geoff forever questioning why. Geoff did not know what happened. Sven was right beside him one minute and gone the next. The wind was blowing a billowing, haunting smoke of war. Geoff could feel something right before it happened. Then nothing. Nothing but darkness and emptiness. Nothing that felt like peace.

Geoff had taken a good hit to his brain. He had a piece of shrapnel the size of a pizza slice. The military doctors had no choice but to take some of what they could out and place a metal plate on the right side of his brain. The family was told that the results might be grim.

But they did not know Geoff Santrew. He was a tough lumberjack and the best workingman around. He was not going to give up. His family prayed day and night. Now, Geoff Sr. was not keen on praying, but Bertha said she knew that in his heart he prayed for the son who had followed in his footsteps.

Geoff Jr. was placed in a sedated coma so that his brain would heal. Slowly, they brought him back from the ominous world of darkness. Later, he would say that he saw a light that brought him to a vision of Christ himself. He said that his conversation with Christ confirmed that his time was not yet at hand. He had a few more things he had to do on Earth.

When he woke up, Geoff was astounded by how much just the name of the Lord brought him immediate peace and tranquility. He had a long road to hoe, but with the help of his family, he was able to recuperate in less than a year. Dottie knew that Kenworth was hiring, so the next step was for Geoff to apply.

He wondered if he would really be a candidate for hire. Had his newfound faith come to wavering again? Right before he opened the car door, he saw a sign that said, "Need engine builders of heavy-duty engines." *Thank you, Lord,* emblazoned not only on his heart but also in his head. Geoff was given a second chance at life and he went with energy balls to the wall. No one was going to tell him no. He was going to build a bridge of communication that no one could ever destroy, not even a great tragedy.

Boundaries are limitless when one puts a prayer and a mind to it. That is just what Geoff Jr. did. After six months on the job, he was promoted to supervisor of the assembly line of engines.

## The Girl of His Dreams

To celebrate, Geoff and his friends went into Seattle to eat and see the young ladies of the day who might just allow their hearts to skip a beat or two. They went to Pier 51, Iver's Fish Restaurant.

Before Geoff could even order, a beautiful brown-eyed woman stood before him who stole his heart. He knew the moment he set eyes on her that this was the woman he would spend the rest of his life with. Diane didn't know whether to laugh or walk away. She felt her heart skip a beat. She was nervous yet excited that this young man with the deepest blue eyes and wavy brown hair was intent on pulling her to him with his smile.

The song "Harbor Lights" was playing. The lights on the dancing floor were low. Geoff Jr. took a deep breath and walked over to the woman of his dreams.

29

"I was just wondering if you would mind being with a veteran who thinks you are the most gorgeous woman in this place. Ma'am, would you like to dance?"

As the story goes, the rest of the evening was the beginning of the rest of the their lives.

Geoff Jr. and Diane married on December 9, 1947, in a small wedding. Diane's little sister, Beatrice, was the maid of honor. Geoff Jr. had asked his father if he would be his best man. Geoff Sr. was taken aback and humbled at the honor. How could this man who had never asked for anything and had followed every order he ever gave him, both when little and now, ask him to be his best man? He humbly—perhaps the most humbled he had ever been—accepted with tears glistening in his eyes.

The rest of the story was built on love, laughter, and life.

# THE SEA OF
# REMEMBRANCE

The open demonstration of love did not come easy for Kevin. He had learned the boundaries of his culture early on. His mom and dad demonstrated outward love openly. But that was short-lived, for when Kevin was seven, his parents were pulled from this earth on Labor Day 1958, in a boating accident in which Brian, his brother, was the only survivor.

Kevin remembered that day like yesterday. The day started off cool and calm. His parents, Diane and Geoff, were excited. They were taking the children to LaPush and the Nisqually River. Brian and Kevin could hardly wait.

"Kev," Brian said. "Do you think we should take the slingshot to shoot rocks along the sound later?"

"No! We are going boating today. How could we possibly shoot rocks on the boat? Boy, and you are older than me! You sure don't think!" Kevin joked and ran away so Brian couldn't catch him.

"You just wait. I am going to bury you in the sand, and then let's see who is thinking!"

They both laughed as they went to the black 1957 Ford Fairlane, their dad's pride and joy. He couldn't afford the true whitewall tires, but that did not stop him from placing imitation whitewalls on the black tires. Besides, no one knew that they were fake unless you went up to the tires and peeled the whitewall away.

As they got settled into the car, the neighbors were also getting into theirs. Kevin's family and the neighbors, Steve and Monica, were quite close, who had no children of their own. Kevin and Brian were as close to them as their own children would have been. The families ate together every night. One night would be at his house, and the other night would be at Steve and Monica's. The families never tired of one another.

The destination was excitement in itself. The outing took the family to the Nisqually River, which emptied into the Pacific Ocean. The boys loved driving through this area because the Nisqually Indian reservation was located on the route to the river. The Quillayute Indians were known for reverencing the natural environment, particularly salmon and red cedar. Geoff Jr. always told the boys that the Nisqually Indians were entitled to all the steelhead salmon in the rivers and basins around the reservations.

The boys dreamed up wonderful adventures of securing all the salmon. They thought that if they could get all the salmon, their parents would never have to work again. Then there would be more time for fishing and boating. This kept them busy for the short jaunt to the river.

However, when they arrived, Kevin had a stomachache, but he did not want to tell his parents because he really wanted to spend the day on the boat. The boys had talked about this day for weeks. Each day, they dreamed of what would happen on the boat. They talked about who would catch the most fish and what, of course, would be the greatest catch of all, though they did not know the population and specifications of the fish they might see in the waters. Undoubtedly, each boy was prepared to accept the crown in glory, even if neither of them knew the ropes nor had the expertise that came with being a king catcher commandeer.

The boat was Kevin's father's joy. It was an aluminum Willie boat for drifting and light boating and not the greatest to look at. However, it brought joy to the family because there, on the water, there were no financial worries. The family was together, and that was the important thing, for family time was limited.

Kevin's parents were almost ready to launch, but Diane, being a natural mom, knew something was not quite right with Kevin. When she asked what was wrong, he caved in and told her that he had a stomachache.

Geoff Jr. wanted Kevin to go, but Diane felt better with him staying back with Monica after she had given him some Pepto-Bismol. Kevin hated the taste. Worse was the fact that he could not go on the boat. He stayed on the beach with Monica. As his family left with Monica's husband, Kevin laid down on the blanket stretched out before him. There would be other times that he could go out with his family. Maybe, he thought, God would even let him stop having stomachaches. Slowly, as the sounds of the gently rushing tide of the ocean ebbed, Kevin fell asleep.

Suddenly, he was awakened by a commotion. Monica was crying. "What happened?" he heard her say.

The police officer looked over at the innocent boy. "Take Kevin, and meet us at the hospital."

Monica grabbed Kevin and they went to the hospital. There the sad news was too much for Monica to take. She collapsed into the arms of the police officer. Her husband, along with Geoff Jr. and Diane, were gone. Taken too soon from this earth. Drowned in the deep, blackened waters of the Pacific Ocean. A contributing factor was the cold water.

How could this have happened? Where was Brian? All Kevin could think about was where his mom and dad were. Where was his brother? He began to cry and felt alone when he saw his aunt Dottie walk in along with his aunt Beatrice and her husband, Otto. When Kevin saw Beatrice, in a state of shock, he ran to her and screamed, "Mommy!" At that moment, Beatrice and Otto knew that Kevin and Brian would be theirs. They would have to stand in for the parents who were taken too soon from this earth.

Later, it was found out that the boat had capsized. Since the family did not have enough money to buy lifejackets for everyone, the one they had on board was for Brian. Geoff Jr. had told Brian to throw his body over the hull of the boat. As Brian was pushed to shore, he drifted in and out of consciousness. When the coast guard found him, he was fine except for exhaustion, fear, and a feeling of emptiness. These are the boundaries that Brian had put up and would live with for a long, long time.

After the funeral, the boys went with Otto and Beatrice to live in Minnesota, back to where the farm was. The bridge of family was connected again. But that underlying feeling, which is treasured by people could be swept away in a moment. Would this be swept away as well? Surely, through the eyes of a seven-year-old boy that was how it was perceived.

It only took an instant for a thick wall to develop around Kevin's heart. And it would take many years, perhaps a lifetime, for the boundaries to be thinned. Life has its ways of constructing bridges, destroying them, and connecting them again.

# LOVE, WHERE IT
# ALL BEGAN

I was reminded of my boundary and where it began.

My mother's parents came from Damascus, Syria, to the Land of Opportunity. Mom's mother was named Mineera Hanna, who I called Teta. She was twelve years old when she was given the opportunity to come to the United States of America. Barely a teenager! Her parents had agreed to a matrimonial arrangement with my grandfather, Dematah Zehabeen. He was fifteen and thought he knew everything about being a man and a man of honor. Thus, as a man of honor, he looked to the agreement as the foundation for his future. I marvel at the wonder of matrimonial agreements. While humanly these two people would never match, God knew what he was doing.

The marriage arrangement took place in Damascus. Life was not easy prior to coming to America and getting married. My grandparents had not known each other personally in Damascus. My grandmother came from a line of seamstresses, who spent their days only imagining what life would be like if they were rich. No, not rich like a princess, but rich like a secretary. Her dream was to be able to read and write.

The cobblestone streets of Damascus bore the footsteps of my grandmother when she was little. After her chores of the day were completed, she would take long walks, imagining the freedom of one day going to school and actually becoming someone— anyone—other than who she was. Her dream was to write the story that God had put in her heart. That one day the words would be written on paper until those same words danced in the hearts of every reader. But that was not the case. Females were subservient to the males. Girls and women were placed in the role of caretaker of house and children. It was not only their job but also their duty. In those days, to belong to a large family was to have riches in the legacy of families, whereas coming from a small family did not give homage to that family.

When the news came to Teta, she was not overly thrilled. The aspects of marriage were not her desire. As a young, poor Syrian girl, the dream of an education was far from reach. Her only hope was to journey to America, the Land of Opportunity. But she reluctantly agreed, for what other choice did she have?

Teta told me that she had just three weeks to prepare. On a dreary spring day, she bade farewell to her family as she departed with her cousin Gabriel. Looking over her shoulder, she saw her mother waving with tears in her eyes. The date was April 1, 1912. It would take at least a week to arrive in England in order for her to board the Titanic.

They were to ride the Baghdad Railway, boarding at Aleppo, Syria. However, they did have a car, bought by bartering with neighbors, that was started by a crank. The roads were bumpy and the driving uncomfortable. After the arduous journey, they arrived in Tartus, Syria, at 9:00 p.m. Gabriel was exhausted. Teta, so it is told, did not want to travel and begged to go home. Gabriel said to her in almost a fatherly manner, "Absolutely not. You are under a marriage agreement. We are Zaheeban. We do not break contracts!" She knew in her heart of hearts that this notion was impossible. Still, while the journey ahead was adventurous, the road behind was melancholy. She already missed her family.

They arrived at the boarding house, fatigued from the week's travel. When they walked in, Teta and Uncle Gabriel were not prepared for what came next. The innkeeper explained that the Baghdad railway to Aleppo was not due until the next day, which would put them behind schedule to get to the Titanic. While it sounded good to the young girl, Gabriel was distraught. *But God still has a plan,* he thought. *Our God is sovereign, and he will make this right.* This in and of itself brought promise to the new journey.

# THE LEGACY CONTINUES

My grandmother had a heart for everyone in Brooklyn. She raised her nine children by the ways of the old thought, like if you are too tired to run after them, tie them down before you give them a spanking. And by George, that is exactly what she did! Nevertheless, her children loved her. No, not just loved her. They adored her. Her sweet aroma of security carried down to her grandchildren.

Teta loved to cook as well as garden. She always wore dresses. Some called them housecoat dresses. They were the kind that tied around the waist. They reminded me of hospital gowns but with just a wee bit more color and flow.

You never saw my grandmother looking untidy. Her apartment was the same way. She always welcomed visitors. She would say in her broken English, "If we have floor space, we have enough room for everyone." Yes, my Teta was the pillar of hospitality. She was also a Proverbs 31 woman, a woman of noble character.

> Her husband has full confidence in her and lacks nothing of value. She brings him good, not harm, all the days of her life. She selects wool and flax and works with eager hands. She is like the merchant ships, bringing her food from afar. She gets up while it is still dark; she provides food for her family and portions for her servant girls. She considers a field and buys it; out of her earnings she plants a vineyard. She sets about her work

vigorously; her arms are strong for her tasks. She sees that her trading is profitable, and her lamp does not go out at night. In her hand she holds the distaff and grasps the spindle with her fingers. She opens her arms to the poor and extends her hands to the needy. When it snows, she has no fear for her household; for all of them are clothed in scarlet. She makes coverings for her bed; she is clothed in fine linen and purple. Her husband is respected at the city gate, where he takes his seat among the elders of the land. She makes linen garments and sells them, and supplies the merchants with sashes. She is clothed with strength and dignity; she can laugh at the days to come. She speaks with wisdom, and faithful instruction is on her tongue. She watches over the affairs of her household and does not eat the bread of idleness. Her children arise and call her blessed; her husband also, and he praises her: "Many women do noble things, but you surpass them all." Charm is deceptive, and beauty is fleeting; but a woman who fears the LORD is to be praised. Give her the reward she has earned, and let her works bring her praise at the city gate. (Proverbs 31)

Yes, as I always read that, I think of Teta in all her humbleness and beauty.

Now my grandfather was a different story. He was short and wide. He rarely smiled, but you knew he loved you. He could not read or write. His goal was to one day be able to sign his name in English. While he did have some difficulties, he was a responsible father and grandfather. He had a little clothing store up on Fifth Avenue named after the first grandchild in our family, Martha. The name was as delicate as my cousin, Martha's Mercantile.

Every day, Jiddo would put on his dark gray pants, white shirt, overcoat, and, yes, that derby hat. He thought that wearing the hat would make him feel and others think he was important. He rode the bus every day to and from his store. As we grew older, as a rite of passage, we were allowed to work in his store on Saturdays. Jiddo's love for us came through the gifts he gave us.

On Valentine's Day, all the daughters received candy. On Mother's Day, all the daughters received bras (he got them real cheap on Canal Street if he bought by the bulk, which he did!). At Christmas, everyone received musty sweaters from his store. (These were the sweaters that no one else wanted to buy.) Yet in the midst of this quirkiness stood a man who loved his family. We knew he loved us, but he did not have the emotional tools to let us know how much he loved us. That would come later.

# THE LITTLE GIRL
# WHO ALWAYS CAME
# WITH A MESSAGE

It was getting late and still I felt the churning of memories in the pit of my heart. "Lord," I prayed, "make that thought go away." But it just lingered like the dew of water after a shower. Why was it that I felt such emptiness in these last weeks and days? Again, the little girl came to my mind. What was she trying to tell me?

In the days of old, Gabriel was an angel who was a messenger from God. Was it God sending Gabriel in the form of this little girl? What was the message? As I pondered on this, I felt my body relaxing.

So much devastation had happened to our country. Yet I prayed that the healing would come. I wanted to understand the wrath of evil over our country. I also saw the other side. Not all Middle Eastern people are cruel. The culture that I embraced was one of love, understanding, and nurturing. It had its holes within its foundation, but then again, so does every other culture.

Once again, I was reminded of the angel Gabriel. He had the arduous task of telling Mary that she was holding Christ Jesus in her womb. He would be the baby who would be born to save us. The baby that she would hold would one day hold the world. He was the messenger of God to bring the impossible to the possibility of thinking. If this was the case, and it was, did Gabriel now represent the little girl in my visions? I wanted so much to understand. I wanted to shout to the world that a bridge needed to be built in order to bring peace to all mankind. Peace was the only solution to the destruction and ruin of this world. Who was I to think that I could accomplish this feat? Who was I to make the world see the wrongdoing wasn't from one entire culture?

As I looked out the window one last time, I saw the moon. The moon in its entire splendor brings God's creation of light to a dark and dreary environment of devastation. I began to pray and feel myself falling into a deep sleep, hoping for a bridge of communication to end the sorrow and devastation of so many people and lives. As I fell into a deep sleep, I was surrounded by many moons of hope.

## Fast-Forward

As I gazed out the window, I saw a city desolate in its tragedy. Why would someone or some organization take the lives of so many Americans? Were they trying to make a point? Yes, all over the world the point was underlined. The reason for the attack? The fact remains that Al-Qaeda saw America as its audience. They wanted to make sure that the terror they brought to our land would undoubtedly make its mark. In the Al-Qaeda regime, overcoming America is the gold medal of terrorism. They want it all. After all, aren't we the country that is the land of the free and home of the brave?

My heart ached for the thousands of lives that were destroyed in minutes. Where was God in all of this? My faith didn't waiver after 9/11, but feeling safe in my own country did. If Al-Qaeda could do this, what makes anyone think that it won't happen again?

Thoughts ran rampant through my mind. *I am tired, Lord. Tired of the pain of my own people summoned to the world of guilt and bringing war on our own American soil.*

What was it that keeps troubling me? It was as if something or someone continually followed me, letting me know I have a job to do. No, it was not the professorship at the university. No, it was not being a wife to my husband. There was something I was supposed to be a part of. But what?

My thoughts were cut short as Kevin unlocked the door. I looked forward to him walking through the door. He was my rock. As I went to embrace him, I was reminded of how safe and secure I was in his arms. I felt alive. Yet I always carried the burden for others, even if I didn't know them. I always took everything in life to mean that I was a part of the happenings of the world. It didn't matter that I was far away. I was connected to everyone and every event that happened, especially when it involved the Middle East and my culture. I felt solidarity to America. After all, I am American. Yet, I also felt solidarity to my background. Kevin knew this. He knew my passion for my people. Still he stood beside me as my strength, protector, and best friend.

Kevin had had a rough day at work. I saw his frustration. How could I help? "Kev, would you like a glass of wine while I finish up dinner?"

He smiled and looked into my eyes. It was the same look that swept me off my feet when I first laid eyes on him. "That might just do the trick. A little relaxation and I might be in better shape than I think."

That was my man. The simple things in life made him happy. While we ate, we enjoyed each other's company and shared the happenings of the day. I didn't tell him about my apparition or vision. He might think I really had gone off the deep end. Or that perhaps I truly was not right in the head.

After dinner, Kevin sat in his favorite chair and watched the late news. As I washed the last of the dishes, I looked at the TV. Again, I saw this little girl, motioning me to come. My first instinct was to scream. My second instinct was to yell at Kevin and tell him what was going on. However, the third instinct told me to find out what was making this little girl appear and why.

As she motioned, I saw something in the background. Its shadow loomed over a circle. I looked closer at the circle. I saw a carousel like the one in my childhood that I had ridden so often. Was it the carousel at Coney Island?

# AROUND, AROUND, LOVE ABOUNDS

Daddy had been home for almost three weeks. Every day was like a new day with him around. John, Lizbeth, and David went to parochial school. It was a Catholic school. Sacred Hearts Church and their school were right down the street from Nona's, who was John, Lizbeth, and David's Italian grandmother. My school was right across the street from our brownstone, so I was always the first to get dismissed from school. Nona lived in a brownstone just a couple of short blocks west of ours on Hicks Street. Daily, after checking in with Teta and Aunt Salima (Mom was at work), I usually scooted off to see Nona and wait for my cousins.

Nona wasn't my grandmother per se, although she might as well have been. She was a grand lady. Her braided gray hair hung all the way down her back. She was of tiny stature and a beauty in her own right.

One thing that I loved was when she let me take the dough from the inside of the Italian bread and dip it into the spaghetti sauce she was making. This was a daily routine. She always served pasta with whatever she was cooking. But she saved the best for me, the dough in the middle! After I ate it, she would put meatballs in the space in the bread, which was sort of like a pocket bread.

Always at three on the dot, David, John, and Lizbeth came bobbing up the stairs.

"Hey, kiddo!" John would say. "Meatballs again?" He would smile at his Nona as she gave him a small hero sandwich.

One day, Uncle Paulie came home early. He announced to us, "Guess what? "We are all going to Coney Island. Yep, that's right! So run back to the house and get your best on. Jack and I are taking you." Jack was my dad and Uncle Paulie, who was like my second dad, was John, Lizbeth, and David's dad.

Wow! I was so excited! David, John, and I raced to our house, but Lizbeth took her time. She had to put on her makeup and, of course, perfume. Sometimes the perfume got to us, but most of the time, its scent was sweet. She was a teenager now, after all.

As David opened the heavy wooden front door, he bumped right into my dad. Being the jovial guy he was, Dad said, "Do you need my glasses to see where you are going?" Sheepishly, David told him no. Needless to say, he was truly sorry. Daddy just told him that it happens to everyone once in a while. He then informed us of the great excursion we were going to take, and on a school day no less!

The women were not too happy, though. They had cooked dinner for us, but in their quiet, calm manner, they caved in. They stayed behind while we all ran to the Rambler. It was roomy, but with four excited kids and two adults, it seemed quite confined.

Off we went. It wasn't just an excursion of sorts. Uncle Paulie cranked up the radio to the voices of Frank Sinatra, Patsy Cline, Doris Day, and others, and off we rode singing songs. Our favorite one was "Side by Side." We weren't rich by any means, but when we were together and singing, we felt like queens and kings. Uncle Paulie and Dad always made us feel like that on these special trips.

We couldn't wait to sink our teeth into a Nathan's hot dog and some French fries. Suddenly, Dad said to Uncle Paulie, "There shouldn't be any traffic here on Ocean Parkway this time of day. What do you think, Paulie?"

Uncle Paulie scratched his head and turned to look at us from the front seat. "Well, we have nothing to do but to give these kids fun, so let's just patiently wait. Don't sweat the small stuff. It will all turn out okay."

So in the meantime, we didn't think. We entertained ourselves with Uncle Paulie taking the lead, singing Frank Sinatra songs. The time flew by so fast!

Coney Island never wore out its welcome to us. We always looked forward to going as if it were the first time. Truth is, we went at least one-gazillion times. And each time we were excited.

When we finally got there, we all had to relieve ourselves, so that took at least fifteen minutes. First thing after that, the serious activity was to drag Daddy and Uncle Paulie off to Nathan's for a good old-fashioned hot dog. John, of course, was known as the messy one, and his ketchup ran all over his shirt. Thank goodness Daddy had a shirt in the back of the Rambler. Yes, it was a little big, but it fit the purpose and saved the evening.

We spotted the ride that was our all-time favorite: the carousel! The horses looked so regal, and we jumped on them and rode away. Closing our eyes, we felt like the wind was beneath us as we galloped in circles!

We were like that as a family—a circle that could not be broken. Uncle Paulie and Dad were best friends, but more importantly, they were brothers in a family that, bound by culture and honor, brought them together. We were so happy and blessed. Both dads were home and our favorite ride proved what family was all about. We went home happy, exhausted, and full.

Our dads, our heroes, that is what it is all about. They protect us, and our security lies in their arms. We are safe. There, no harm can come to us or the people around us.

# THE THREADS
# OF A FAMILY

As I look back, I see what strength families have. Through trials and tribulations, families stick together. That was how I grew up. We stood by our heritage and took pride in who we are.

I think of the threads of trees and the threads of family. My mind wanders and ponders, thinking of the threads of family. A tree takes root in the ground of life. When nurtured with love, culture, and morals, branches begin to blossom and expand. Each branch is different yet contains the same ingredients: love and life. Each branch connected to the same tree continues to grow, at times with strife, at times with peace. Leaves grow and fall, like people who move away or who have gone home before us. But the leaves that fall from above become the nutrients for the tree. Once again, the leaves give back to the family, just like family members who reconnect and give back to the family.

You can tell the age of a tree by a cross-section of its trunk. Each circle represents ten years. You can tell the closeness of a family by the people here and those not here who hold us close in their hearts and prayers. Like the newly formed circles in the cross-section of the trunk of a tree, the circles of the tree never end. And the circles of our families never end. A family builds on the foundation and, like a tree with deep roots, stands firm and strong and calmly endures through disasters and brokenness. As water supports and sustains the tree, the blood that runs through a family supports and sustains each member.

When crisis arises, our family is there; when love abounds, our family is there. Our youth holds our memories. The present becomes the memories of our golden years and the beginning of memories for our children. Our future lies in the peace of knowing that we are loved and sustained by God and a solid tree called family.

# THE VISION

"What are you thinking of, Michie? Your mind is a thousand miles away." Kevin looked at me, intent on searching for the reasons why my thoughts were distant.

"Kevin, have you ever had a vision? I mean a vision that is a sequel into something you were supposed to be involved in and it actually came true?"

Kevin grasped my hand. His hand was my protection from the fear that sometimes overcame me. What if …?

"Of course there are times in my dreams that I see something and the next day when I wake, that scene comes into play," Kevin said. "But they are just dreams. Freud, as you may remember in the psychology courses, would interpret dreams."

I stopped him. "No, Kevin. I continue to see my past coming back to me, reminding me that I am yet to do something important."

He looked into my eyes with a love I felt in my heart. "Michie, you *have* done something important. You have your doctorate, you teach, you write, you are involved in the community."

I was beginning to see that Kevin did not understand what I was trying to tell him. *He will think that I am nuts. Why is it that sometimes he just doesn't think beyond logic? Or maybe I am the one who is illogical.* Bringing my hand to my face, I assured him that he was right. Subject dismissed, at least for now. But I still felt the nagging of my heart and remembered the little girl at the corner earlier. Perhaps I just needed a vacation.

"Come into my chambers, and we will discuss this." Kevin stood and gently took me into his arms, reminding me of the security he gave me. We walked to our room.

The night with Kevin always brought me peace and love. I fell into his embrace as we connected our hearts and bodies.

# MORNING

Morning. A new day, a new creation. A time to restart the button of life. I thought of Psalm 143:8: "Let me hear in the morning of your steadfast love, for in you I trust. Make me know the way I should go, for to you I lift up my soul."

"Michie, I will give you a call later, okay?" Kevin always tried to calm my nerves. And most of the time he did. He hurriedly kissed me on the cheek. I was astounded by how much I loved that man.

"Sounds like a plan, hon. Be blessed today, and remember I love you up to the moon, around the stars, and back again."

Morning is a time to reflect and recharge. Lord knows that I was trying, but there were so many thoughts on my mind. The family, my husband, the little girl, and what my mission was. How could I stop my mind from running rampantly?

# Morning Sun and Evening Rain

I arrived at the office just in time to see Suzie, my colleague, getting ready for the day. Yet she was more than my colleague. She was my yin in the educational arena. Suzie was from Puerto Rico and kept me laughing when I didn't have any laughter in me. She was the head of the math department. Her personality would not lead one to think she was a math genius. Suzie had that New-York-mixed-with-Spanish accent. If you talked to her on the street, you would have thought that she had a menial job, if a job at all. But she could fool you. She was the life of the party. The minute you talked to her you got the energy of life. She was intelligent and yet could reach the common people of the community. I marveled at her. I sometimes wished I were like her.

Suzie had two daughters and was expecting her third. My dream, my hope, was to one day share the joy of parenthood with my husband. It had been five years and I had still not borne fruit. One day …

"Hi, Suzie. What's new?"

"What's new? Well, I haven't lost any weight yet." Suzie looked so cute as she pranced in a circle like a duck. "But in one month, I will proudly lose at least eight pounds, sista! Maybe a miracle will happen and I will lose even more. Gotta run. Pre-Cal is calling. Remember we have lunch before the faculty meeting. That is, if nothing else is on your agenda." Suzie laughed and left.

Suzie knew that my schedule was tight. Tighter than I liked. I had strived to be where I was. But now, all I wanted was to have a child and be full of oatmeal, complaining to Kevin that I had no time for myself. My thoughts wandered to that little girl again. *I have to stop this or it is going to drive me crazy.*

I had twenty minutes before my first class. Today was the history of the demoralization of Middle Eastern women. What a topic! *Has this world demoralized us? Or has the world worked so there is more to a woman than what meets society's mind?* A topic to consider, and I pondered it. I glanced at the clock. Fifteen more minutes to myself.

Something caught my eye as I turned my chair to the window. It was broad daylight, and again, there was that little girl. *Why does this happen? What is God trying to show me?* A thought came to mind: *He loves you in the morning sun, unconditionally without regret, boundary or absolution, He is there.*

The little girl was holding an umbrella and dancing in the rain. Now I truly was convinced that I was losing my mind. What on earth was my mind doing to me? I truly needed to make an appointment with a therapist if this continued. But the thought once again diminished as I saw the time and hurried to my classroom.

I venture to say that I was idyllic when it came to the servanthood of women. I walked into my classroom, only to be accosted by a broom. *Wham!* The broomstick hit my head and I blacked out for a second. I couldn't believe I didn't put that away. The janitor should have, but he had called in sick and I felt that the least I could do was sweep the floor for him before I left yesterday. But this … *Okay, restart button, Michie.*

My students were there, ready for any knowledge I could give them through my lecture or our discussion. I believe that a true teacher is like Socrates. No one is above or below knowledge, so sometimes a teacher can learn from her students. Having an open mind makes facilitating a course so much easier.

I had ten male students and nine female students in my class this semester. I loved to teach, but more so, I loved to learn from my students. They had the vitality I used to have. Energy to learn and eagerness to conquer the world.

Today's topic was the "Stoning of Soraya," the tragic story of how a man can so easily do away with his wife (Sahebjam, F. 1994). I emphasized to my students that this story is true. It is a story of an innocent woman who did nothing but take care of her two sons and was below the auspices her husband. The location of this horrific tale takes place in the village of Kuhpayah in Iran. The story is told through the account of a journalist, Freidoune Sahebjam, whose car had broken down in the village. He tells of a woman named Zahra and her failed attempt to save her niece, Soraya, the day before from stoning. Zahra wanted the world to know what had happened to her niece, and the journalist had the courage to tell it.

As the story unfolds, Soraya's husband, Ali, accuses her of having an affair just so he can get out of the marriage contract. Undoubtedly, this was not an easy thing to proceed, so he needed evidence. Therefore, he invented a story that Soraya had been unfaithful. This would give her husband freedom from having the burden of child support if he were to divorce her because of unfaithfulness.

Eventually, as told by Zahra to Sahebjam, they found witnesses who were threatened with their lives if they did not comply with this story. Once the witnesses agreed, Soraya was dragged through the streets by her husband. He wanted to show how hurt he was, so he beat Soraya publicly. This prompted her aunt Zahra to step in to defend her. But naturally, in the realm of sharia law, she was convicted, and though her aunt tried her hardest to flee with her, it was for naught.

55

The hardest part to comprehend was that Soraya's own father disowned her and was given the first stone to throw. However, he repeatedly missed. Was this a sign not to carry out this horrible act?

Her husband, infuriated, took up the stones and began the fatal ritual. He forced his two sons to partake in the stoning of their precious mother. The crowd joined in, and when they thought she was dead, they stopped.

Then Ali saw that Soraya was not dead, and he continued stoning her. She suffered a sad, painful, unjust death. A death of an honest woman, innocent, without a chance to speak her mind. How wrong was this?

I felt that this would be an intense discussion. I took a deep breath and asked God to give me wisdom. "Okay, class, let's get to work. We ask ourselves, women and men are equal, aren't they? Or do we still have barbaric systems, especially for women in this world? In the Middle Eastern countries, sharia law still exists under Islamic rule."

Sam, a brown-eyed, six-foot tall student, posed the question, "What is sharia law?"

"Okay, Sam. Let's go over this again." I smiled. He was so young and eager to understand how Islamic culture differed from what he had grown up with.

"I come from a Middle Eastern family that is Christian. The laws for my grandparents were different from what I grew up with as a child in America. Here we have rights equal to men." There was snicker throughout the classroom. "Yes, even though we all know that forty-three years ago women protested in New Jersey against the Miss America Pageant, claiming that bras, girdles, and the like were instruments of torture to women, I believe that we now have more equality than we did. Some say in today's standards it is men who are demeaned. At any rate, let's get on with the review of the demoralization of women in the Middle East.

"I know that we are not reviewing just for Sam. Isn't that right, Sam?"

Sam broke into a boyish smile. "Yes, ma'am. You got that right," he said in his Southern drawl.

I continued. "In the Middle East, personal status law is discriminatory with regard to parental authority, marriage, and the consequences of breaking the marriage. Let's take Syria, for example. Fathers are deemed the head of the household."

Sam interjected. "That seems to be okay, right? I grew up that way."

I smiled. "Yes, Sam, but in this case, women do not have a say necessarily the way your mom does. Let's continue. Here in America, we have parental rights. But in the case of divorce, unless the mother is a child abuser, the court looks favorably on the custody of the children to mothers. The court also grants fathers some percentage of custody (IHRDC, 2013).

"However, Muslim women are usually granted custody of sons until they are thirteen and daughters until they are fifteen and lose custody if they remarry. Now while some mothers wouldn't mind that because they say teenage years are the hardest, this is the reality of the law. Under certain laws, both parents have equal guardianship rights over children during marriage. But if a couple separates, the father is offered custody first and then the mother."

Elizabeth, another bright student, questioned this. "How can fathers work, clean, and get homework done if they have to care for the children? Isn't that appalling when the women go out and work and then give the fathers child support?"

Again there was laughter. "That, my dear, is another topic. Shall we go on?"

I went on to tell the class that Muslim men can divorce without the agreement of their wives, but Muslim women do not have the same right. Rather, women seeking a divorce can only obtain one according to limited criteria, such as the husband's illness or desertion, or can obtain a *khula* divorce if they renounce their

57

dowry. But women in Syria aren't as adventurous for freedom, shall we say, as men. Therefore, the rate of divorce is quite low. And yes, divorced women are traumatized because of the stigma that divorce carries. Furthermore, divorced women may not be awarded citizenship to children born to non-Syrian fathers.

"Does that clear up some of the questions in regard to Syria?" I was sure there were still discussions to be had, which we would have later. "Okay, let's take a closer look at the codes of sharia law and women before we have those discussions, shall we? Remember, too, that these discussions are not limited to that of Syrian women. We will encompass within our discussions the demoralization of women of all areas within that region and elsewhere. This and the next session of class we will be talking about sharia law and how it affects women. The question will remain, As a world, do we still see the demoralization of women, which invariably will bring the destruction of families and ultimately countries?"

Elizabeth spoke up. "Of course it is. There are facts that consistently ring true. Don't you agree?"

"Yes, Elizabeth, and we have to look at those facts and still try to understand that we have come so far as a nation but not as a world. Okay, class. Enough for today. Our next session will entail our looking at the penal codes of sharia law as well as another case of abuse. See you on Wednesday."

The class spilled out into the light of the rest of the day. I wondered how much it would take to see our world change so that we would honor and respect both males and females.

I looked at my watch and remembered that I had to meet Suzie for lunch. As I cleared up my books and notes, I looked to the back of the classroom and saw once again my girl. Funny how I was now saying that she was mine. *Lord, what is going on? Are you trying to tell me something?*

I tried to gather my thoughts as I walked in the direction of lunch. Suzie would get me laughing, and I rested easy in knowing that this too would come to pass. I was thinking that the confusion about seeing a little girl would all be clear soon. I would find the wisdom behind it.

As I walked, I contemplated what was it about her that intrigued me. Sometimes when I saw her, it was as if there was a peaceful rain flowing around her. A mist of sorts. Evening rain when all is soft and quiet. Evening rain, when the problems of the day flow out softly as the drops hit tenderly on the night.

# IT'S RAINING! BUT THE
# BOAT WON'T SINK

We were bored. It was Saturday, April 23, 1966. I knew that the poem my teacher read, "April Showers," was now true. I couldn't believe it. We were supposed to go to Prospect Park. How I loved going to Prospect Park! I felt like it was our playground alone.

It was also a place where the Battle of Brooklyn was fought. I remembered hearing that in my third grade class. My teacher, Miss Walker, told us it was a place that helped make our city important. The story went that George Washington was fighting in the Revolutionary War right here in Brooklyn. Our army was called the Continental Army. Its troops held the English soldiers back long enough for George Washington's group to escape from Prospect Park all the way to New Jersey. Of course, it was not called Prospect Park then. It was known as Brooklyn Heights. Well, it was something like that anyway. I loved the history that our first president stood right where my feet did whenever I went to the park. It is a very special place.

John always made fun of me for loving history. He said that history is history and will always be a mystery. One day, I am going to show him, though, that history is *not* a mystery. You just have to read a lot to understand it.

Anyway, John wanted to sail his new boat that he had made in the pond. I thought that the boat would immediately sink. So did David. We laughed when John showed it to us. He had to build a boat for his Cub Scout badge. It was known as the "milk carton boat." John worked constantly to perfect it. He had asked me to bring home empty milk cartons from school, the small cartons that we had every day at P.S. 29, the school that I went to. It was right across the street from my house, located on Kane and Henry Street. I only had to walk a little way across and then I was there. Teta and Aunt Salima could look through the window and sometimes see my class!

John asked me to bring the cartons home was because at his school, they poured milk right into a glass. They didn't want to spend money on cartons that people could throw away, I guess. See, John and David went to Sacred Hearts. Lizbeth went to Bay Ridge High School. Sacred Hearts was a Catholic school. Of course, I wasn't old enough to go to Bay Ridge High. I didn't even wear makeup yet. I wasn't allowed to attend Sacred Hearts because I wasn't Catholic. That was okay. My religion was Eastern Orthodox Catholic.

There were things that I did not understand. Like, for instance, why Lizbeth got to wear a pretty white dress and veil, like a bride, but I couldn't. Mommy always said it was because when I was born, I was given the gift of Jesus's death and resurrection along with my baptism. This made the difference. I had the gift of being allowed to drink the wine and eat the bread. The bread was specially made. It had a cross shape baked into it every Sunday!

Communion always came around 10:00 a.m. on Sundays. I was usually hungry, so I was glad about that. When I received the bread, it tasted like honey. It was so good. I always liked the taste of the wine, too. I knew it wouldn't hurt me because the church wouldn't give it to kids if it would hurt them. It was supposed to be the symbol for the blood of Jesus.

John, David and Lizbeth, though, had to wait until they were in second grade for their Communion. In fact, this was the year that David was going to make his Communion! I was excited about that. He had to wear white too! But not a veil, of course. He had to wear a white little suit. When he tried it on, he looked so cute!

61

David was chubby but cute, and like my baby brother. I always wanted to protect him, especially from John. But John wanted to always protect me. That is, unless we were fighting. We really only fought over things like whose toy to play with or who was going to get the longest piece of taffy. Even when we fought, though, it lasted only minutes.

Day after day, John would work on his milk carton boat. He would cut the milk carton in half so that it looked like the bottom of a boat. The boat could go two ways. It was like a sailboat with a motor. He made the sails out of colored drinking straws and paper. The paper was supposed to be the cloth of the sails. When that was done, he designed a motor.

It wasn't really a motor that needed gas. He made it with paper, rubber bands, and paper clips. He would tighten the rubber bands around the paper clips, and when he let the paper clip go, the rubber bands loosened like a fan, propelling through the air!

Being that it was raining on this day, we decided to use the big bathtub in the basement to see if it would really float. I thought for sure that it was going to sink. David and I bet that it would sink; after all, it was made of paper. I had $2.50 in my piggy bank, Mr. Bojangles. He was so cute!

Daddy loved to dance, and he said that I could move my feet just like Mr. Bojangles, who was a real smart soft-shoe dancer and didn't let anyone put him down. He lived in the 1800s and kept on pushing people about letting him dance. My dad always told me that he could dance a real good tap. I was real good at tap and tried to live up to Mr. Bojangles, I guess because he was strong and brave. In the 1800s, people didn't take kindly to tap dancers who were considered different. Daddy said that Mr. Bojangles was not different from other people. He just had a different skin color. So I named my piggy bank Mr. Bojangles because he was so shiny and different. His skin color, which was the color of a copper penny at noontime, shined brightly!

Mr. Bojangles was made of glass. However, he always had a shiny pearl-like glow to him. Sometimes, if you turned him a certain way, Mr. Bojangles looked like he was made of rainbows. He had a slit on top. I guess Mr. Bojangles was a strong bank because it was so hard getting money out of him once you put it in.

Anyway, I was all in for winning the bet. John said if he won, he would take my 250 pennies. I turned to him and said, "What happens if you lose?" John laughed. "Look, Michie. I am not going to lose. But if I do, I will do all your homework for one week."

John was real excited that David and I had bet my money. But that was okay, since he was like my brother.

John carried down his sailboat with pride. You would have thought that he had built the Titanic. The boat sailed! I was so upset because I would have to break Mr. Bojangles. John could see how upset I was, as a tear started to roll down my cheek. But I wanted to hide it.

"Michie, you really don't have to break Mr. Bojangles.. Let's just call it a cousin's bet. After all, I am the winner and I can decide what I want." He looked at me with the love of a brother. "How about a piece of that gum you have at home instead?"

I jumped up and hugged him as tightly as I could. I was so happy that I would have Mr. Bojangles forever that when we got home, I gave John the whole pack of gum. A cousin's bet is a cousin's win, and that's what he wanted.

How I loved my cousin at that moment. I also told God that I would never bet something as special as Mr. Bojangles ever again.

We tried the pennies on the boat. If placed the right way, John knew it would work. Although, I must say, David and I had our doubts. John placed three pennies on each side, making sure it was balanced. David and I tried to keep our doubts to ourselves. Would you believe that it worked?

I was so proud of John and of all of us. We had worked together as a family. Success! John may have earned the badge, but we all earned the satisfaction.

# Justice or Hatred

It was time to review for my class in the morning. Wednesdays were always rough for me. I got my books, sat down on the couch, cozied up with a blanket, and began to work.

The research was interesting. The topic was restructuring society on the basis of violence and sexual separation. I was entertaining the thoughts of the Islamic Republic of Iran and the penal codes. As I reviewed, I realized that the penal system is one of the main conductors for installing and sustaining such a society and administration.

The foundation of the Islamic penal codes is a social doctrine based on sexual apartheid. The Islamic people look at the belief that women are defective in their natural potential and abilities. Furthermore, men must be superior to women and women must submit to their husbands in a way that is harsh.

The Islamic penal codes have inflicted huge injustice on women. However, they have also been where women have stood up against the regime in every possible way with some victories to their credit. It is no exaggeration to claim that women have inflicted the greatest defeats on the regime in the realm of culture and "public morality and chastity" and its symbol, the Islamic dress code, or *hejab*.

Some of the articles of the penal code are incorrigible. One can imagine a situation where a boy of fourteen and a girl of nine steal. According to the law, the girl would lose four fingers of her right hand for the first offense, her left foot for the second offense, prison for the third, and execution for the fourth, whereas the boy would go free as a bird!

Another example of inequality is in relation to the murder of a child. If a father or paternal grandfather murders his child, he will not be subject to *qesas* but will be subject to paying blood money to the inheritors of the deceased as punishment. A similar crime by the mother will be treated like an ordinary murderer, subject to *qesas*. The law recognizes the right of parenting over the life of a child and grandchild for the paternal side of the family but not the maternal side.

My heart continued to ache for the women of the Middle East as I prepared for my class. I looked outside and wondered if there was so much darkness that one cannot distinguish that God is turning away from our world because of all the injustice. We are all his children and yet there is such evil.

The Islamic punishments have motivated and birthed a culture of violence against women, especially within the family, and that violence has seeped into violence against children. The knowledge that men receive a lighter punishment if they commit violence against women undoubtedly encourages such violence. Stoning to death for adultery, although can be given for both sexes, has been carried out mainly against women. Newspapers are brimming with details of wives, sisters, daughters, and children murdered. The family has become an institution of violence.

The harm to women is a travesty. There is so much injustice. Yet our world continues to allow this to occur. Even after years of the Islamic regime in power, the administration tries to obscure these laws from the general public, for they fear its anger. When demonstrations are reported against stoning, there is a thread of understanding that there is resistance, with women at the forefront.

A majority of religious women, even some who have a stake in government, find themselves alongside secular women in this opposition. For over twenty-five years, women have tried to break the rules related to the dress code (*hejab*). Tens and hundred thousands of women have been arrested and given extreme punishment for going against the *hejab* laws. Women have strongly faced their punishments, which sometimes included seventy-four lashes, rather than submit to a backward and anti-women culture (Gender Equity, 2014).

These laws in their entirety are more in keeping with a society still in the age of barbarism. At a time when most countries are banning the death penalty, punishments like cutting off hands and feet, stoning to death, cutting out tongues, and gouging out eyes is totally unacceptable.

All this was getting to me, so I stopped researching for a while. How could this world allow this? Where is the primary focus for human rights? Certainly not for women. Looking out the window, I knew that I had to continue and finish before Kevin got home.

A story as horrible as Soraya's is that of Sakineh Mohammmadi Ashtiani (Yong, 2010). Ashtiani was born in Tabriz around 1967. She grew up in the rural town of Osku located in the East Azerbaijan Province of Iran. Sakineh worked outside her home for two years as a kindergarten teacher.

In 2005, Ashtiani was arrested on charges of adultery just like Soraya, as well as for accusations of conspiracy to commit murder in the death of her husband. In 2006, the court sentenced her to death by stoning after she was convicted. Her children, Farideh and Sajjad Qaderzadeh, initiated an international campaign in hopes of overturning the sentence. They wrote a letter about their mother's case, which was published by *Mission Free Iran*.

Many prominent media sources picked up on the news via interviews with her sons that included information on her stoning sentence. The international publicity generated by Ashtiani's situation led to numerous diplomatic disagreements between Iran's government and the heads of specific Western governments. As a result, her execution has been stayed indefinitely. However, shortly after the international campaign began, various Iranian officials stated that Ashtiani was also guilty of various charges related to the murder of her husband that included murder, manslaughter, conspiracy, and complicity.

However, major human rights organizations, such as Amnesty International some NGOs, and her lawyers stated that Ashtiani was acquitted of murder, and that she initially received a ten-year sentence for complicity in murder and "disrupting the public order." It was reduced to five years on appeal. She was convicted twice of adultery in separate trials and sentenced to death by stoning. In December 2011, the Iranian authorities indicated that they intended to go ahead with her execution, but by hanging.

However, the hanging was not carried out, and Iranian officials afterward denied that they had intended to execute her. Her fate remained unclear until Ashtiani was pardoned for being a good role model in prison.

Praise God! Jesus knows the hearts of women all over the world. The travesty against them is horrid. Yet the question remains, How can I do anything?

Kevin walked into the door, and with that I put my books away. Wednesday morning would be here soon enough. I would enjoy the treasure of love and being with my soul mate for tonight.

However, as we retired for the evening, I hoped that the questions that I would pose to my students would emblazon their hearts.

# Questions or Answers to a Journey That Never Ends

"Wednesday morning. Rise and shine, sleepyhead." Kevin kissed my neck and reminded me that I would be late if I didn't get going.

I kissed his forehead. "You have an internal clock for waking me up, which is why I never have to worry about the power going out. You will always be here to get me going." He nodded and smiled mischievously.

I rose, showered, and dressed in a matter of twenty minutes. Off to the knowledge race. "By, hon. I will see you tonight."

Class was on time today. The students were eagerly waiting for the discussion.

The question that I posed to my students after explaining the stories to them was this: What kind of lunacy is this? A man thinks he can dissolve one family so to bring up another with a new spouse. Or a woman is condemned when she has done nothing? This is not the world I grew up in!

The discussion among students was an interesting one. Jason, a strapping young man in the back, brings up an interesting point. "The Middle East is the Holy Land. Why is it that they have a hard time honoring one another? Doesn't God tell us that wives are to honor their husbands and, in turn, husbands are to honor their wives as they honor the church?"

"Jason, you are right when we speak of the Middle East and the Holy Land, at least in my understanding. After all, this was where the Lord, for those who believe in a man called Jesus, lived and died and rose again. However, this is not the holy ground for women. Women are treated as less than second-class citizens."

I glanced at the clock. "Okay, your assignment is to research and find a human rights story in the Middle East that involves a woman. Next week, we will gather in a Paideia Seminar and discuss what we have researched."

I explained to the students what Paideia Seminars and Socratic discussions entailed. Discussions among professors and students should be one that allows for the students to be active stakeholders. A key feature of Paideia Seminar is the question design. Rather, the way questions are crafted and sequenced so that there is an important difference between Paideia Seminar and Socratic discussion.

Imagine an hourglass. The first question is relatively open, as participants are asked to identify the main ideas of the discussion. If notes are given to the students, the questions are narrowed down in focus, which require close analysis of textual details. Toward the end of the seminar, a question is posed where the participants are asked to personalize and synthesize the ideas. In other words, the closing question is opened back up in terms of possible correct responses.

Take, for example, a question set on the preamble to the US Constitution. The opening question could be "What is the most important word or phrase in this text?" Students have many choices for their response and are invited to express their personal preferences. Similarly, the closing question for this text might be "In what ways does the preamble relate to your daily life?" Notice how the aperture narrows with these core questions: What do the authors mean by "domestic tranquility"? What is meant by "general welfare"? Why is that important?

In a Paideia Seminar, the opening and closing questions give students time and space for personal connections. While these questions are relatively more open, they always relate to the ideas in the particular text. You could say the opening and closing questions help build community, while the core questions push intellectual rigor.

Consider the impact of this combination of seminar questions. The shape of seminar is driven by question design. In other words, the seminar is deliberately planned to help students feel human connections while critically thinking about the text.

As I ended class, I saw Rachel lingering behind. Rachel is from a town in Iraq called Tutakal. There, she witnessed young women who had to succumb to female circumcision. A blue tattoo on her chin tells the story of this cultural norm. Her hometown culture felt that if a woman were circumcised, it would cut down on her sexual activity. It was, and is still, barbaric. Rachel had four sisters at home in Tutakal.

"Dr. Santrew, I understand what you are trying to teach and instruct us. However, the students in this class will never know how deep the suffering of women in the Middle East really is. They are subservient to the men around them. They walk but in fragmented bodies. They don't have rights." Tears filled her eyes. "Girls are not honored as individuals or as humans who can make a difference. My own sister was slaughtered in an honor killing."

In the Middle East, women are often killed for marrying or having relationships not approved by their families or because they are perceived to have somehow dishonored their family. Rachel began to shake. I put my arms around her to let her know just by my touch that I understood, even though I didn't and couldn't even fathom the atrocity.

"Rachel, all I can do is to continue to teach from my heart. I, too, am Middle Eastern and know of the atrocities that still occur. That is why I teach the courses that I do. I am here for you. I know this is little consolation. But I am here. You can come to me anytime to talk. Please know that I am not only your instructor, but I am also your friend."

She looked at me through sad brown eyes. "I know. That is why I am here. There is an orphanage on the outskirts of Tutakal, as you know. Many little girls are there. I don't know how I can help, but I am here to emplore you to join me to help. I don't want the girls to be hurt. One of them is my niece. She is four years old, the daughter of my sister. I am here in New York and still part of a world that is barbaric. What can I do?"

My heart palpitated. Could this be what I had seen of the little girl that followed me? "Rachel, we will look into what we can do. I can't promise, but I do know that I am connected to you. Please know I am here to help. Now go; dry your eyes and your heart. We will manage this the best way we know how. First, we pray and then we act. Okay?" Here I was, telling someone who had grown up under the Koran to pray. What was I thinking?

Rachel let go of me. "Thank you so much. This is for you." She handed me a note. It read, "نظر قلبك وأنا أعلم أنكم سوف يساعد,"

"Rachel, I can't read it. What does it say?"

Rachel again looked up into my eyes, searching for something beyond. "It says, 'Your heart is seen and I know that you will help. ul-lah al-must-a-an.'" With that, she turned and walked out the auditorium door. *What was that she said at the end?* I thought. *I will find out.*

My thoughts were consumed with Rachel, and how my heart ached. If only I could have just captured those little ones in my arms. *If ... no, I can't think of "if." I am not in a position to even think of adoption. But if I can't have my own child ...* The thoughts ran rampant through my mind.

I hurried home, for Kevin was waiting. *A little girl to have as my own, to play with and to walk across life's bridge together. No, not possible. Or is it?*

# My Sister Is
# There to Stay

"Okay," Lizbeth said in a rather superior tone. "You think you are so smart. You know that photograph of the college girl your mom keeps telling you is your cousin? Well, let me tell you something. She is your sister, Silvie."

I was eight years old. "What are you talking about? I don't have a sister. I wish I did. Then she would knock you down, like I am going to do right now." I pushed Lizbeth into a chair. Where did that strength come from? After all, she was older and stronger than me. She pushed me back. At that moment, could hear my Aunt Salima coming. Lizbeth started to spout out that I started it when, she saw that I was crying.

"What is going on here?" Aunt Salima want to know.

Why don't you ask her!" I looked at Lizbeth through tears. Before I even had the chance to finish what I had to say, Lizbeth chimed in.

"Mom, you know how Michie is! She believes everything, even when it is a joke!"

I couldn't understand Lizbeth. It didn't seem like a joke. Mom didn't tell stories. "I am going back upstairs, Aunt Salima! I am going to ask Mom right now!"

Aunt Salima tried to stop me, but I ran from her grasp. It took less than twenty seconds for me to fly up those stairs. And a lifetime of wanting a sister. Maybe, just maybe, Lizbeth was right.

As I got to my apartment door, I quietly walked in to find Mom sewing as usual. She worked so hard. One day, I would help her. She was such a good mom. I knew that life was hard for her. All she really ever wanted was to give me all I wanted. What did I want now? A new sister! But I knew that would never—

"Michie, hey darling. What did you do downstairs? Are you three tired of each other? I only have a little more sewing to do on this pretty ballet skirt for your recital."

"Mommy, it is a tutu. It is a French word that means bottom. That is what Miss Minerva calls it." I walked over to her and hugged her. She was my mom. There was nothing she could do to be less than perfect.

"Oh, pardon me, Miss Ballerina!" We both laughed. I put my arms around her and hers fell gently around me. "Mommy, you know my new cousin Silvie that you told me about? The one in the picture?"

Mom looked me sincerely in the eyes. Her eyes were so big and sad sometimes. Now she looked at me with a look that I may have asked a question that was more than a question. "Yes, honey. What about her?"

I walked over to the windowsill. I loved Kane Street with all the noise, love, and peace that went with living in an Italian and Middle Eastern neighborhood.

That was, except for Mrs. Fitzsimmons, the busybody of the neighborhood. She watched us, well, I should say, she watched *over* us when we left for school and when we came home from school. She was a good woman but always told our moms and dads what we were doing. She just sat and rocked on the top of her stoop and watched.

"Well, Lizbeth said that she is my sister and not my cousin. How can that be? I mean, she never lived with us, and you don't have pictures of her except that little picture. Mommy, Lizbeth is wrong, right?"

Mom at first didn't know what to say. "Come. Let's go sit under the fruit bowls." The fruit bowls. That meant business. Whenever we sat in the living room, I knew we were going to be serious.

We went into the living room and sat on the couch, which was under the fruit bowls. Actually, they weren't really fruit bowls. They were sculptured into the walls. Aunt Agora, the artist of our family, had come a few months earlier and painted them. The gold in the bowl was almost real. You could just reach out and almost pick the fruit and eat it. That was how real the colors were.

"Michie, Silvie isn't really your cousin, darling. She is your sister. You see, Daddy married another person before me. It was many years ago, and he had a daughter. When he went to the war the first time, his wife and him drifted apart. When he came back from the war, well, they weren't happy anymore. So he decided to get a divorce. He had to leave them, and he couldn't take Silvie with him. It broke his heart. He was sad for so many years. That is, until you came along. He loves you with all his heart and soul. You are and will always be his little princess."

I couldn't believe my ears. I had a sister! "Mommy, Mommy! I am so happy! God heard my prayer and gave me a sister, and a big one at that!" I could not contain my excitement. I jumped up and down and twirled around. I jumped so high and so hard that I almost chipped the fruit bowl on the wall.

"Michie, Michie, calm down. I have never seen you so happy!"

I finally sat back down on the couch. "Mommy, don't you see? I really do have a sister. I don't care that she doesn't live with us. I don't care that Daddy was married before. I don't understand it all. But I do understand that God gave me the miracle I have been asking for ever since I was little!"

"My darling, you are still little," Mom said as she hugged me. "You will always be my little princess."

I hugged her back. "I know, Mom, but I am bigger, and that is why you waited to tell me, right?"

Mom, I am sure, thought that I would be upset and feel abandoned at the thought that I would possibly have to share her and Daddy with someone else. But I couldn't have thought otherwise. "I am going downstairs right now and tell Lizbeth thank you! I have a sister!"

Mom couldn't contain herself any longer. "Wait, Michie, wait!"

# THE MIRACLE OF INNOCENCE

I was intrigued by what Rachel had asked me. She wanted help so badly for her family.

Every day we read in the paper how children are separated from their families due to the ravages of war. Children who have seen with their own eyes their families torn apart by the bullets of hate. Their mothers and fathers standing beside them one minute, giving them security, love, and warmth, and then in the next minute swallowed up by a pool of blood, oozing hate. Why? Why has this world come to this? What happens to the children and their siblings?

I couldn't think. In my mind, I saw eyes of children looking at me, questioning if they even had an hour of life left, much less tomorrow.

Rachel was right. Something had to be done, but what? What could I possibly do to help her plight? How could I give life back to the eyes of the innocent?

Just then the phone rang. It was Suzie's husband.

"Michie, she had the baby! She had the baby! I am so excited!" Juan couldn't contain himself.

"Oh, I am so happy for you, Juan! I know that you will love her to life." But I couldn't conceal my envy, though small. That in itself hit a raw nerve. I remembered my early days in college when I thought I was pregnant. I went to the doctor to see if I truly was. Back then they didn't have self-pregnancy tests. I had misgivings, but I was so excited. I thought at the time that that would have resolved any issues I had with Keith. That he would say, "No problem. We just get married." I was young and foolish to think that such a thing could create a marriage when there was no commitment on Keith's part.

It had been a brisk day for New York. The temperature was just right. Autumn was my favorite season. The season of warmth glistened for rest in hopes of a serene spring. I was in my first semester of college and thinking that my world was just beginning. I had an appointment with Dr. O'Hare at 1:30 that afternoon, but I had time to walk around Prospect Park, which was and always has been my safe haven. The park I went to from the time I was a little girl.

I had an hour or so to kill, so I walked to the lake that is in the center of the park. The air smelled like warmth amongst a colorful breeze. The colors of the oak trees beckoned so that you could encircle yourself within their leaves. I continued to think about being a mom and Keith, my husband, my child's leader. I stood back in the shadow of the tree and prayed, "I speak according to your Word, O God, that … I have been blessed with a baby that is encompassed within a healthy and *fruitful* womb! I say in Jesus's name that I have conceived and I am pregnant! Every part of Keith and me is to come in line with your Word, Jesus. I realize that Keith does not know you the way I do. However, you will function efficiently, the way you were created to, fearfully and wonderfully made."

I also prayed for good, solid attachment of my baby to the uterine wall and then for my baby to grow perfectly and be nourished and protected for the full nine months. I plead the blood of Jesus as a hedge of protection around my womb, protecting my baby from all harm. I declared this in Jesus's name, as the Word says, "Ask whatever you wish in Jesus's name and it will be done!" I gave God all the glory for my healing and for my baby, ending with "Let it be done according to you, O God!"

I didn't realize that the time had slipped by while I was in communion with the Lord. I looked once more at the autumn warmth of the oak tree and hurried out of the park to my destination. Dr. O'Hare's office was just a few blocks away. The brisk air felt good on my face as I tried not to conceal my joy.

Mrs. Smith, the secretary, was stoic as I gave her my name. I don't think she ever truly smiled at a patient. I don't know, but something inside told me that when she was younger a great sadness had been birthed. I told myself that I would keep her in my prayers and thoughts. *Maybe, just maybe, one day I will see that youthful exuberant smile on her sad face*, I thought as I sat down.

There were three women in the waiting room. Two of the women were in their twenties, close to my age. The third woman looked tired and drawn out. She was a brunette in her late thirties. One of the younger women asked her, "Is this your first?" The older woman laughed. "No, honey, this is my fifth and final one, I hope. Having five babies in eight years is a little too much, but a smile from an infant is worth a million dollars at the end of the day. Besides," the older woman continued, "my mom had ten!"

*Wow!* I thought as I thought of my mom. She could only have me, and I was blessed because of her. She wanted more children but could not have any. Every step of life that I took, she celebrated with me. From the time I could remember, Mom was always there. She always told me, "Your son is your son until he takes a wife, but your daughter is your daughter the rest of your life. I will always have you, Michie. Thank you, and I thank God every day for you." Tears filled my eyes.

It seemed odd. My mother should have been with me, yet how would I ever have told her? The thought of a baby in my arms was miraculous. I never really thought of my being a mother. However, deep inside, the love of my own baby was exciting. And with Keith, nothing could be impossible. But my mom knowing that I had a child without a commitment, without marriage, would surely have broken her heart.

Suddenly, my thoughts were silenced. "Miss Handee, Dr. O'Hare is ready for you. And how are you today?" Shirley was always pleasant, even for those appointments women faced daily with Dr. O'Hare. Going to Dr. O'Hare was something that came with being a woman.

I had gone to Dr. O'Hare since I was seventeen years old. I had endometriosis, which is a disease with no cure. Even the brightest of stars cannot possible see the darkness of that disease. I had hurt with it since I was sixteen. At the time, there was nothing that could be done. My diet was changed in hopes of feeling better, but to no avail. I took painkillers, but soon the pain was too great and the medicine too weak. My mother and I researched, and I started going to a support group, but the women were older than me. I decided I was going to fight like a girl with backbone. Over time, I had learned to live with it. But it was always there, though. Many times I wanted to shout, "Just because you can't see it, doesn't mean it doesn't exist!" But day after day, I got stronger and, in time, learned that this entity, endometriosis, was part of me, part of my life.

Then a miracle happened. I met Keith. He understood my pain and knew how to make it go away through his gentle touch and loving words. Lately, though, our relationship had turned. I didn't know what it was, but we weren't getting along.

Each time I went to the doctor over the previous two years, I dreaded it, for I knew the outcome. No children. Keith really didn't want a commitment. He knew my heart. I loved him with every breath of life. I swooned at his words and felt like a teenager on her first date. Yes, Keith was my first love. The man I wanted to spend my life with. He, on the other hand, was becoming distant, quarrelsome, and restless. He always told me, in one way or the other, "I love you, Michie, but love isn't like the earth that is just there. It is like the wind that blows gently through the spirit." No, I wasn't happy—especially when I had to see the doctors.

79

This time, however, I was ecstatic. "I am doing great, Shirley. I just might have some news after this appointment."

She looked at me and smiled. "You might be young and you know you have your future ahead of you. It may happen or it may not. Time and testing will tell. The main thing is that you know you are beautiful and you are an innocent creature of habit. But if that is what you are desiring, a baby, then I am happy for you."

Dr. O'Hare interrupted us with a knock. "Knock, knock. How are you today, Miss Handee?"

"I am fine, Dr. O'Hare. Just fine."

Dr. O'Hare was a sweet doctor. He was in his mid sixties and was a country bumpkin, of sorts. He came from a town in Mississippi or, I should say, city. Hattiesburg, Mississippi, to be exact. He had a Southern drawl that could charm a snake right out of its skin. He was a kind spirit too.

"I see that you are not due for your exam for another three months. What brings you here today?"

"Well, I think that I may be pregnant. I am not sure, though. I haven't had a period in two months. I thought it might be nerves; you know I am stressed with my schedule and work." I had taken on two jobs. During the day when I wasn't at school, I worked at Saint Stevens Hospital. At night, I worked at the bookstore on Fulton Street. In between, I attended the university, not sure if education or nursing was going to be my major.

"You know your condition, Michie. Chances are you are not, but it does happen. Miracles happen every day. Well, the first thing is the first thing. We will have to run a pregnancy test to see for sure. That should not be a problem, dear."

He told Shirley to get the urinalysis cup. I was a slight bit embarrassed. I knew the outcome of a woman having endometriosis. I should have known if I was pregnant or not. Shirley must have thought that I was a woman of no smarts. In this day and age, women took precautions. But my precaution was my endometriosis.

Shirley directed me to the restroom. "Oh, God," I prayed. "Let this be a miracle to bring Keith and me closer, to bring us to a commitment." After I finished, I left the restroom and told Shirley that I was ready.

"Okay, Miss Handee. Dr. O'Hare will be just a minute or two." I smiled. Keith was going to be so happy. I didn't know how I should—

Again my thoughts were interrupted. Shirley looked a little more serious this time. "Dr. O'Hare will be right here. You just sit tight."

"Thank you, Shirley. I am fine."

Dr. O'Hare came in, and he, too, looked serious. *What is going on?* I thought. *Could it be twins?*

"Michie," Dr. O'Hare began," I am afraid that the pregnancy test came back negative."

My heart stopped and my thoughts raced. *How could that be? I haven't had my period for two months!*

"What you have, Michie, is what is clinically termed pseudocyesis. This condition allows you to believe that you are expecting a baby when you are not really carrying a child. People with pseudocyesis have many, if not all, symptoms of pregnancy, with the exception of an actual fetus. This unusual condition accounts for one to six out of every twenty-two thousand live births."

Dr. O'Hare continued. "When a woman feels an intense desire to get pregnant, which may be because of infertility, repeat miscarriages, impending menopause, or a desire to get married, her body may produce some pregnancy signs, such as a swollen belly, enlarged breasts, and even the sensation of fetal movement. The brain then misinterprets those signals as pregnancy and triggers the release of hormones, such as estrogen and prolactin, that lead to actual pregnancy symptoms.

"I am sorry, Michie. I think that you indeed have these symptoms. You know we have talked about this before. You have severe endometriosis. The chances of your getting pregnant are unlikely. But there are alternatives. You are young and vivacious. Don't think about it right now. Go home, enjoy your life, and in time, your miracle will come. Other than that, I will see you in two months, fair lady."

I could hardly contain my tears. "Thank you, Dr. O'Hare. I quickly got dressed, paid the copayment, and walked briskly away from my dreams.

*How could I have thought that I was carrying Keith's baby? What if I had been? Now that I am not, what's next?* Keith and I had not been getting along for quite some time. I thought if I was pregnant all the quarrels would have taken a backseat to a baby. How could I have possibly thought otherwise?

The tears flowed and flowed. Dreams of reconciliation between Keith and me were shattered. He would never understand what I had just gone through. As I walked I knew that my disease was debilitating. Even If I could get pregnant, which I wasn't, I knew somehow that, no matter what, Keith and I would never be a couple again. Not now, not ever. The furthest thing from his mind was marriage with someone he quarreled with.

As I turned the corner, I unexpectedly ran into a young woman with her baby. That baby was beautiful with sparkly eyes. Searie was just six months old, yet there was an old soul about her.

"Oh, Suzie, I am so sorry. I didn't see you! I just came from—"

Just then Searie started laughing. I looked down at her. Her sparkling gray eyes were laughing and showing me the innocence of a child.

"It is okay, Michie. Where are you going or coming from?" Suzie was a neighbor and a good one. She had a little girl named Inez and now little Searie.

"I just had a bad day, that is all. I am sorry again if I hurt Searie's walk."

Suzie shook her head. "My Lord, girl, it is okay. You just take care of yourself, okay? Hey, by the way, I decided my major is going to be education. Math. What about you, Michie?"

"I haven't decided yet. I figure I better get through the Foundations of Education course first before I decide."

Suzie hugged me. "All right. Well, I am here if you need me. I need a crazy partner like you to go through school with. You keep me sane." Her laughter balanced me.

*How does Suzie do it all? A young mother in her early twenties, a husband, and school.* I had things to look forward to, but not with Keith. "Okay, Suzie. See you soon. Love you."

Now my thoughts drifted back to the present. Keith had been long out of the picture, and my knight in shining armor had taken his place, my husband, Kevin. Yes, a beautiful, wonderful, and godly husband.

"Michie, no, you don't understand. We have a son!"

A son! Suzie said she was having her fourth girl. How could that be? "Juan, I am so excited. It is a miracle! Suzie thought you were having a girl!"

Juan was floating through the phone. "I know, I know! How a miracle happens like this, God only knows. I mean, I would have been happy with a fourth girl, you know. But now I have a Little Leaguer to play ball with and go fishing with. The little rascal is going to catch some big fish with Kevin and me!"

I was crying tears of joy for Juan and Suzie. Yes, the little rascal would catch some big fish. He would be a son not only for Juan and Suzie but also for Kevin and me. My heart will always want a child, but my body says no. I feel joy but also pain—like a butterfly stuck in a cocoon, never allowed or given the opportunity to emerge.

# My Sister My Friend

The road was winding around the mountain as we drove through the night. Stars glistened liked eyes filled with curiosity. I was going to meet my sister, Silvie, for the first time! I couldn't sleep for all the excitement in my head!

"Daddy, how much longer?"

Dad chuckled. "What's your hurry, Squirt? Silvie is not going anywhere. Now hush. Lie down and sleep until the sun smiles."

Mom was fast asleep in our Rambler that Dad had won. He belonged to the VA and had paid dues. One night when he was working, a phone call cried out in the dark. Mom is deaf, so she could not hear the phone. It scared me half to death, though. I jolted out of bed to answer it.

"Mommy, Mommy, the phone is ringing! You have to answer it!" I handed her the receiver.

She was barely awake when the voice on the other end said, "Ma'am, is your husband, Jack Handee, there?" She looked at me because she couldn't understand what the voice was saying. I shook my head no. She had a curious look on her face. "Well, ma'am," the voice continued, "we are calling you from the NCO club. Your husband just won a 1965 Rambler!"

Mom finally had heard the voice. "You are kidding. This must be a joke. We never win anything!" She was now standing, straight as an arrow.

We were both so surprised. Dad wasn't home. He was working at Fort Hamilton. He had won a car!

"What do I need to do, sir?"

The voice went on to explain that all Dad had to to do was sign papers the next day.

"That easy, huh?" Mom asked, not sure if this was on the level.

"Yes, ma'am. You be blessed in your new car, okay?"

Skeptical though she was, Mom felt the excitement and miracle build, I could tell. "Thank you. I don't know how to thank you. I will believe it when I have the keys in my hand."

"Yes, ma'am. I know it feels like a dream. Good night now."

"We won! We won! Our worry over driving is over!" Mom was singing in a way that I had long since forgotten.

That's how the Rambler became ours. It was silver, the color Dad always liked. It had four doors with a 440 motor. Dad's pride and joy. He polished it once a week. Now, as we were driving to see my sister, the sister of my prayers, new to me, I looked up above. I saw the stars had that same shimmery glow as our car. I closed my eyes and almost immediately fell asleep.

When I opened my eyes again, the sun was coming through the window, welcoming the new day. I popped my head up. "Are we there yet, Daddy?" I knew Dad could tell how excited I was. I had waited so long for this dream that I thought would never come.

"Yes, honey. We are almost there."

I could tell Mommy was tired. But even though we had long left our home, God could tell, as I think anyone would have, that we were content and excited.

My stomach made a silly sound as a sign that it was time for breakfast.

"What is that rumbling in the back? I am sure it is the clock of hunger." Daddy laughed. He knew that I hated when my stomach made that noise. But all I could think about was my sister and pancakes.

"You know what's calling, Daddy."

"Indeed I do, Squirt. The pancake house is just a little up the way."

After a delicious breakfast, my stomach was happy.

We pulled into a gas station near Silvie and George's house. I wanted to make sure that I looked good when I met my sister for the first time. Mom braided my hair and put a pretty pink bow in it that matched my outfit. Something nice and simple. Dad then called Silvie to say we were on our way.

I couldn't believe my eyes. When we pulled up, there was a yellow sheet that said, "Hey there, Michie! I have been waiting for you all my life!"

Daddy beeped the horn, his way of saying we are there. It wasn't polite, but I think Dad was nervous too. It had been so long since he had seen his first daughter. He always reminisces about it.

I remember it clearly. It was a Saturday. The phone rang, and I answered it. The woman on the other end asked, "Is this Jack Handee's house?" I said, "Yes indeed." She asked if she could speak to him. I gave Daddy the phone, and he listened. Then when he hung up, he cried. He didn't tell me until after I knew that Silvie was my sister. The conversation was one to remember for a lifetime.

She had told him that he may not remember her, but she was his daughter and called to see if he would walk her down the aisle on her wedding day. That broke his heart and yet filled the brokenness with joy. His daughter, who he hadn't seen since she was five years old, was asking what every father took for granted. After much contemplation, though, Daddy said he couldn't because Connie, his ex-wife, would be there and he couldn't stomach her. It was a horrific divorce. Silvie, being the godly person she was, understood, but she made Dad promise to come and visit. Daddy, of course, jumped at the chance and said yes. Now that dream had become reality!

My sister and her husband walked out. She looked so different from me. My hair was dark; hers was lighter. I had dark skin; she had snow-white skin. I had a New York accent; she had a soft, buttery Southern accent. Yet I knew beyond my childlike thinking that she was my sister.

She had that sparkle in her eyes like I had in mine. We got it from Daddy, of course. She sang, "Hi-ho, hi-ho, I have a sister now, I know." Silvie was funny, just like Daddy. I guess sometimes I could be funny. And talk! Boy, she could talk circles around me! Well, half circles anyway.

George, my new brother-in-law, was tall and quiet. He was older than Silvie, and anyone could see how much he loved her.

We walked into their home. It was so pretty. It looked like it came out of a magazine. Everything had its own place. I loved Silvie and George even more now that I had met them. They filled the hole in my soul. God was good to me!

When evening came, Silvie cooked up a good old-fashioned Mississippi dinner. It was delicious. It was country-fried chicken, mashed potatoes with garlic, salad, home-style biscuits (she said she had been baking all day), and, to top it off, pecan pie and ice cream! I was in my glory. I helped pick up dishes from the table and helped Silvie clean up. Afterward, we all went into the living room to visit.

I could tell Daddy was happy. Mom was too. Daddy hadn't seen Silvie in oh so long. The last time he saw her she was a little girl. I asked him on the way down why that was.

"Well, Squirt, things happen in life that can't be fixed. Silvie's mom and I couldn't be fixed. God knew the plan. He wanted me to marry your mom. He knew that he could watch over Silvie until it was time for me to come see her again."

That made perfect sense to a ten-year-old girl. So no more questions about that.

Over the next few days, we laughed, danced, and told silly jokes. We prayed too. We prayed that we would always be together, all of us. Even though there were many miles between us, we knew we could each look at the same star at the same time and know we were doing together. That is how family is. Never really apart, always looking into each other's heart.

87

# THE TASK

Thoughts of Rachel continued to race through my mind as I prepared for class. I was so lucky to have a family that loved me. My cousins were like my sisters and brothers, and my aunts and uncles were my parents as well. Like a thread through cloth, we were woven together to create a supported life, but Rachel did not have that. There was a void in her life because while she lived in the land of freedom, her family still suffered in Tutakal. Even in 2003, girls and women were under such a reign of hate and mistrust that they didn't see the light of a new life within the laws of the land that should have been long forgotten.

In my mind and heart, I felt the pain for Rachel that she could not bear herself. How many times do we read of atrocities in the newspapers and think, *I don't know of anyone going through that pain*? Most Americans are glad that the suffering is far away. It is just news, and news tends to embellish what truly is happening. That was what my mother's generation thought—nothing was going on in World War II, at least not what they were saying about the atrocities occurring in Germany. How little do we forget the bad that has happened in the past?

# SHATTERED STEPS
# OF DREAMS

I think of my mom. She too had experienced atrocity: the atrocity of not seeing her dreams come true. She was the oldest girl in her family. There were four girls, including herself, and five boys. She adored her mother, Teta, as I lovingly adored and knew her. But being the oldest girl, my mom had to quit school and go to work in the sewing factories in New York.

Mom was devastated. She loved school. She felt so lucky to have that freedom. But in her first year of high school she had to leave. She was just beginning to understand that dreams could become reality. Instead, she traded her schoolbooks for bus tickets to a sewing factory in Bay Ridge.

Mom would get up early in the morning, before the sun rose, and walk the five blocks to Atlantic Avenue. She must have traversed those streets thousands of times that she could have done so blindfolded. Each day in the wee hours of the morning, she rode the B63 bus up and down the lengthy stretch to get to the factory on Thirty-Ninth Street. Sometimes, she would take the B37 on Third Avenue, the more boring of the two bus routes, or used the BMT R subway.

Once Mom got to work, though, they were other girls her age who were in the same situation—dreams of youth exchanged for responsibility to help support a family with siblings younger than themselves.

Mom had told me many times that she felt good about at least helping. She had empathy for others. There was this one woman, Helda, who touched Mom's heart. Helda was originally from war-torn Brandenburg. She was a Polish Jew. Helda always had talked to Mom about Brandenburg. Sometimes the reminiscing was good, but oftentimes it was so very sad.

As she and Mom reminisced about childhood dreams, dreams that were shattered by the reality of life, Helda gave Mom a glimpse of what it was like to live in Brandenburg before the war. As a little girl, she lived there with her mother, father, and her brother, Mikel.

Brandenburg was nestled on the Haven River in Germany. Helda remembered how she used to love to go down to the lake and play with her parents by her side. Many times she would marvel at the sight of beavers and otters. The beauty of the landscape energized her creativity in hoping one day to become a horticulturalist. Periodically, she told Mom, there would be air raids. Then she with her siblings and parents would run to the shelters that were built for protection of the townspeople as well as for the military in case of bombings from the air. Helda was accustomed to these raids and so were her friends.

The shelters consisted of many tunnels that intersected, perhaps to give it a more communal environment. This maze was located behind metal panels in the walls, which contained bathrooms, a kitchen, storage areas, and a diesel-powered electric generator. The first three thousand people lined up in an orderly fashion would be allowed to file in through a door and enter an air-locked decontamination chamber under the supervision of machine-gun-toting guards. A face behind a glass window would then instruct these lucky survivors to strip naked. After an ice-cold shower to decontaminate, the shivering, terrified masses were then buzzed through the entrance. After this ordeal, each person would be issued a bright yellow polyester tracksuit when entering the fallout shelter.

The walls of the shelter were painted a light pastel green. Psychologists say that this color brings about a calming, stress-reducing effect. Precautions were taken if there was a malfunction with the generators. The engineers had painted the walls so that they glowed in the dark. The phosphorescence was said to last for two hours, in which time the generator could be fixed if there was a problem. However, the air filtration system in the bunker only had the capacity to be effective for two weeks.

The daily ration was one bowl of soup, which was not much sustenance. The sleeping accommodations consisted of bunk beds, assembled from light aluminum scaffolding. There were exclusive bedchambers, which would be shared by forty people. In case of an air attack, it would not take long for alphas to assert themselves. The uniforms that represented class levels were not adhered to as well as they would like to have been.

The bathrooms were the most gruesome part of the shelter. There were a couple of dozen toilets within the shelter. However, one can imagine how inadequate this was for the needs of three thousand people. There was minimal privacy provided by flimsy curtains. People were allotted only thirty seconds of toilet time. In the event of an Armageddon, there was consideration of suicides. Therefore, the engineers utilized non-breakable material with no piping or scaffolding. Even this was calculated to precision (Burian, Al. 2013).

Helda's dreams were torn apart when she was ten years old. It was a bright and sunny day. One minute she was playing with her friends outside, and the next she was running in an actual air raid toward the shelters.

It must have seemed like days had passed, but in fact it had only been five hours since the sirens blasted the beginning of a reign of terror. Her father and mother, were there, but where was Mikel? He was the last to run to the safety of the shelter. Many people were asked, but Mikel could not be found.

When the bombings had finally quieted, all that could be heard was the smoldering sound of silence. Helda and her parents exited the shelter as quickly as they could. The deafening sounds of people wailing who had lost everything heightened the awareness that this was the beginning of shattered dreams. Helda often talked about a bridge she would have loved to see again from her childhood, a childhood with happy memories, but that bridge back to happiness was long ago shattered.

Helda remembered rummaging through the bricks that once held a family, her home. All that remained were the smoldering ashes of a happy childhood. Helda told Mom that when she was rummaging for her favorite comb, she suddenly felt something that brought hysteria to her heart. It was Mikel. He had been killed during the air raid. Mikel, her sweet six-year-old brother. Gone. His little legs never got him to the place of safety. They were blown off during the bombing. Helda's heart broke, and yet her heart would break again and again.

The year was 1933. Helda's family knew they had to leave immediately. However, they were sent to the ghettos in Warsaw, Poland, and were only allowed to take a few possessions with them. They missed Mikel terribly and did not want to leave him behind. But he wasn't there anymore.

Life in the ghettos was far from picturesque. They were tightly woven and overcrowded. Warsaw ghettos lacked electrical and sanitary conditions deemed human. Children suffered the most. The rations were barely enough to keep people alive. The community of the Warsaw Ghetto was given 180 grams of bread a day, 220 grams of sugar a month, 1 kilogram of jam, and 1 kilogram of honey. This did not even suffice for 10% of normal nutritional requirements. If anyone was caught smuggling in food above the ration supply, he or she was executed. Helda's father could not stand this. He wanted to provide for his wife and Helda. He would smuggle in what he could from his job at the factory that manufactured shoes. He loved the smell of leather and the way it felt. Helda remembered her father telling her that life should be like leather, smooth and easy to the touch.

Hitler ordered a barbed-wire fence be put up to divide the Jewish population from the rest of Germany. Later, what was later to be known as the Berlin Wall was built. But that did not stop the flow of love. As hard as life was, Helda still had her parents. This was her safety net. The arms of her mother and father provided security that she did not have since leaving Brandenburg. No matter what turmoil was around her, she was safe because of her parents.

Helda had one friend in Warsaw who was like a sister. Johanna was the same age as Helda. They played for hours on end, pretending that they were mommies. They had one doll each that they had brought from their homes. Even though life was hard, they had each other and their families.

But that all came to an end when Johanna was caught smuggling in food from the other side of the fence. Two Polish women had been tossing packages of food over the fence. This time, however, it fell to the other side. Johanna knew if she held her breath she could squeeze through. What she didn't know was that there was a German soldier standing there.

She begged him not to hurt her. But her cries did not matter and she was silenced. Gone, just like Mikel. Helda retreated after that into her world of hurt. Still, this would not be the end to her hurt but a beginning.

Day after day, Helda had heard of the train. She thought maybe that was the train to freedom. But freedom from what? Death? No. Death was a free ticket to those on the train. Helda experienced it firsthand on December 5, 1942.

It was a grim, rainy day, and the sky told of upcoming snow. German soldiers were rounding up families, telling them they were moving to a better place. However, in order to get there, they would have to take the train. Helda's family was told that on December 5 they would be leaving. They were also told to take few possessions with them. That was easy to do, as they had little they wanted to keep. One particular item was the picture of the family during happier times, one with Mikel.

The train ride was two hours from Warsaw to Treblinka. The train had to cross over the Vistula Bridge. Treblinka was located in a hidden portion of the remote forests of northeastern Poland, along the western border of the Bialystok Province.

When they arrived, they were told they were at a transit camp. Families were separated. Helda told Mom that the women and children were told to move to the left and the men to the right. Then they were told that they had to take showers to rid them of any bacteria. Women had to undress and were forced to run naked along the path of the fence. Helda's mother was quite ahead of her, and Helda saw her push ahead into the showers. That was the last glimpse she ever had of her mother, for her creator and safety net was killed in the gas chamber. When they had arrived at the camp, and her father was told to go to the right, Helda never saw her father again either.

Helda's life was spared because she was strong and determined. She was forced to take care of the clothes of the dead. She was placing clothes in a stack when she found her mother's jacket. All she could do was break down and sob silently into it. Her life was gone.

After the liberation of the camp, Helda made her way to New York and managed to gain employment in the factories.

One thing that Helda always talked about was her feeling on the Vistula Bridge. Once the train reached that portion of the journey, she knew her life as she had known it would never be the same. Her family bridge was broken in Treblinka.

Bridges always link the past. Some go just one way while others extend to the present. And some bridges are best forgotten.

# BRIDGES OF HOPE

"Daddy, can't I sit with you up front?"

"No, Squirt. The expressway is really congested today."

Congested? I thought Dad must have meant crowded. "Daddy, the road is not congested, just crowded. How can the expressway have a cold?"

Mom, Dad, and I laughed and laughed. It was a Saturday, and we were on our way to Jerry's good-bye party. Jerry was going into the army. The family was getting together to bid him farewell. The thought of my cousin going to war never really entered my mind. He was just seventeen, and I thought he was going to be stationed like daddy was at Fort Tilton. But that was not to be.

"Mommy, is Jerry going to be with Daddy at work?"

Mom looked at Dad as if to say, "Give me courage to tell her." Then she said, "Honey, Jerry is going to Vietnam after training. That is where they need him the most."

I didn't know about war except that Dad was in it. "Is it like the war you were in, Daddy?"

Dad's face became serious. He hated to think of the war. "Every war is the same and yet so different. I fought in the Korean War. Jerry is going to be in the Vietnam War. He is going so that we can help fight the ugly guys who believe that freedom should be given by one leader who is in control. Many countries do not believe in the kind of freedom that we have here."

"Oh, okay." That satisfied my curiosity.

We arrived at Uncle Joe's house right when Aunt Agora and her family arrived. I loved it when our family was all together.

Only now we were saying good-bye to one cousin. Jerry looked so grown-up in his new hairstyle. He even looked excited that he was going. I wouldn't have been excited to leave my family. I guessed that things were different when you are seventeen.

In total, there were twenty cousins, from little Joe, Aunt Agora's son, to Jerry, the oldest of the male cousins. Uncle Joe's house was so much fun. He had a trampoline in the backyard, and we all wanted to go on it. Jerry and Ritchie decided that the best way was for all of us to get in line. Most of us listened, but not John and Gabie.

There was a little stream behind Uncle Joe's yard. We always had fun skipping rocks across the stream. I, as John's shadow, went with them to skip rocks. They glistened in the sunlight, and there were so many to choose from. I learned from Daddy that the shape of the rocks didn't really matter. It is how they were thrown. John and Gabie were already throwing rocks to see how many they could skip in a five-minute period. I, however, wanted to get the best rock to skip.

I finally found my best rock. It was smooth and round. Daddy always said that the rock that is the best skipper is one that skips three times.

"You think that you can skip rocks better than me?" John yelled across the stream.

I laughed. "Of course I can. Watch!" I slanted my rock just so. It didn't skip three times but close to it.

Gabie shook his head. "You didn't make it, Michie. John's rock skipped better, cuz."

I was starting to feel my neck get red. I was not going to lose this game! I picked up another rock. This time I remembered to hold it at a forty-five-degree angle. Just as I threw it, I knew it was going to skip three times. And it did! John and Gabie could not believe it. Funny, just when a girl wins, boys always want to change the game.

John decided that we were going to play pirates and that the rocks were our cannons. Well, when pirates want to take over a ship, what do they do? Shoot the cannons, of course. We started throwing rocks at one another, but just so they landed at our feet. We played this game for a little while, each time our "cannons" let out their steam a little harder.

I stopped to watch the sun glistening on a bluebird, whose feathers looked like glassed water in the night, when all of a sudden I heard John yell, "My head! My head!" I rushed to see what had happened. There was blood everywhere. I started to cry because I thought he was hurt badly. And he was, or so it seemed.

My legs could not run as fast as my heart was beating. I had to get Daddy. "Daddy, Daddy! John is hurt! Quick, come here! He is bleeding all over!" I thought I was going to die trying to catch my breath.

Dad rushed to John's side. "Michie, tell Uncle Joe we have to take John to the hospital."

By now all the attention was between John and me running. I found Uncle Joe just as he was coming out of the house. I tried to explain as best as I could what had happened. He met Dad down at the stream, and together they took John to the hospital.

I was so upset. So was Gabie. He didn't mean for John to lose his balance and fall on the boulder behind him. That boulder always was in the way. While I was gazing at the bluebird, Gabie had taken a rock and threw it at John's feet. But before John could get out of the way, he lost his balance and fell backward.

I prayed to God right then and there. "God, if you can hear me, please don't let anything happen to John. He is like my brother. If anything happens to him, I will never forgive myself. Please, God, put angels around him. Protect him and bring him back from the hospital as quickly as you can."

# THE ANGEL THAT
# NEVER FAILS

My Teta, my grandmother, was always there. I loved her so much. Her locks were full of wisdom. Her hair was soft gray with curls that delicately framed her face. Light shined around her face and hair. When I got older, I wanted hair just like hers to show how smart I was.

Teta was always there when I needed her, and even when I didn't. How can I explain her? God does a good job of it. I learned it in Sunday school. This was what I learned through God's Word:

An excellent wife, who can find? For her worth is far above jewels. The heart of her husband trusts in her, she does him good and not evil all the days of her life. She looks for wool and flax, and works with her hands in delight. She is like merchant ships; she brings her food from afar. She rises also while it is still night, and gives food to her household, and portions to her maidens. She considers a field and buys it; from her earnings she plants a vineyard. She girds herself with strength, and makes her arms strong. She senses that her gain is good; her lamp does not go out at night. She stretches out her hands to the distaff, and her hands grasp the spindle. She extends her hand to the poor; and she stretches out her hands to the needy. She is not afraid of the snow for her household, for all her household are clothed with scarlet. She makes coverings for herself; her clothing is fine linen and purple. Her husband is known in the gates, when he sits among the elders of the land. She makes linen garments and sells them, and supplies belts to the tradesmen. Strength and dignity are her clothing, and she smiles at the future. She opens her mouth in wisdom, and the teaching of kindness is on her tongue. She looks well to the ways of her household, and does not eat the bread of idleness. Her children rise up and bless her; her husband also, and he praises her, saying: 'Many daughters have done nobly, but you excel them all.' Charm is deceitful and beauty is vain, but a woman who fears the Lord, she shall be praised. Give her the product of her hands, and let her works praise her in the gates. (Proverbs 31, Bible Gateway Passage)

Every day, Teta woke before even the pigeons on the rooftop of our brownstone. There was a Syrian breakfast that was oh so good. She served zeitoun, which other people know as olives. They were the big black olives that she preserved for us. Teta put vinegar, coarse salt, lemon, and just a wee bit of sugar. Sometimes I wanted them before they were ready. Teta always told me, "They have to stay in the jar for two more days!" But I still tried to sneak one when she was not looking.

Alongside the zeitoun (olives) was kuboos, unleavened bread, and I can't forget the cheese. The cheese was special because it was braided. It was raw mozzarella cheese with anise seeds. You pulled the cheese until it was long and thin like spaghetti, but not quite. You then put it in brine (saltwater) and let it stay for several weeks. It is known as *jibneh mshallaleh.* It took so long to braid it. I had watched Teta do this. Before she braided it, she put the little black seeds in it. Although I now know they were anise seeds, she always called them "seeds of blessings." They give the cheese a pepper taste. I loved this cheese. The braid was beautiful too. Just like when Teta braided my hair.

She spent a lot of time combing my hair at night, one hundred strokes. I think Daddy loved to brush my hair when she didn't because he was preparing my hair to be wise like Teta's. She always told us girls, namely, Lizbeth and me because we lived in the same brownstone, that hair is our crown. That we must always take good care of it. I know that Teta always took care of her crown. Being the Christian woman she was, she stuck hard to the truth of God. First Corinthians 11:15 says that long hair is a woman's pride and joy, for it has been given to her as a covering.

When Mommy wasn't able to feed me, Teta fed all of us. On Sundays, we had family dinner, which consisted of waraq inab, which are grape leaves, kuboos, kibee (we called it wheat pie), rolled cabbage, kousa (yellow stuffed squash), and dessert topped off with baklava. The best was baklava. It was made with lots of honey, and was oh so good!

On Wednesdays, Aunt Salima took over, and we had spaghetti and meatballs or veal cutlets. When Friday came along, Teta made lots of French fries and eggs or fish. We didn't eat meat on Fridays. That was the rule of Catholics. I didn't understand all the rules, but I did love those French fries. John, David, and I ate ketchup with our eggs. Daddy thought that is silly, but we liked it.

Teta was always there. But one day, she had an accident. When John, Gabie, and I were skipping our rocks that turned into cannons, Teta went with Aunt Salima to get grape leaves. But they didn't go to buy the grape leaves. Teta had noticed right before the exit to Uncle Joe's house that there was an unpruned grapevine off the side of the exit of the highway, and she decided it was a good idea to prune it by picking the leaves off the vine. She was wearing culottes, which are like pedal pushers, a flowered blouse, and her sandals. Always looking like a lady, she had to have her culottes loose fitting.

Aunt Salima had driven the car to the edge of the exit. Teta got out to pick the grape leaves. She wouldn't listen when Aunt Salima told her to wait and she would help her get out. It is that stubborn, strong-willed character of hers. Teta had to walk quickly behind the car to get to the grapevine. That was when Aunt Salima heard the screech of tires. A car was coming around the bend too fast and hit Teta. Aunt Salima ran to her mother's side, who was bleeding profusely. The man told Aunt Salima that he would flag someone down to call an ambulance.

Aunt Salima did what she does best, comforted Teta and prayed. From her comfort, Teta smiled the smile of an angel. She knew something was wrong but tried to conceal her worry.

The ambulance arrived in five minutes or less. As they sped to the hospital, they began treating her. First, they had to stabilize her because of her blood pressure. Once they did that, they took X-rays. It seemed that she had a concussion and a fractured rib and needed lots of rest.

Aunt Salima was by her side, and that was a good thing. But unbeknownst to Aunt Salima, John was in the emergency room at the same time! God is all-knowing. Teta was sent to the same hospital as John. Although hurt, she was his angel too. She is always there for us.

Later on that night, Teta was told about John and John was told about Teta. They both had to stay overnight so the doctors could check on them. I guess God knew Aunt Salima needed to save on gas. He is a funny heavenly Father, isn't he?

Jerry's party ended with a bang, a real one for Teta, John, and, of course, Jerry. However, the rest of us were able to kiss Jerry and hug him more because John and Teta weren't there. He knew we were all sad. I prayed that God would watch over and protect him until his return to us. Angels would be around him, I was sure. After all, didn't God give us angels in our family? You betcha!

# ALL IN THE NAME OF HONOR

It was Monday. The sun was trying to shine through the cumulonimbus clouds that danced above me. *Rain? Not until I finish my class, Lord. Please!*

I pondered what Jason had asked me the week before and thought also of Rachel. Honor? Why was there no honor in what was going on in the Middle East or in our country? How could you explain to someone that Middle Eastern families are not all terrorists?

As I walked, I thought of honor and its glory, defeats, and triumphs. I had grown up with honor. There was always an unspoken rule: Honor God. Honor your parents. Love your family. Do good things. Live life abundantly!

Live life abundantly. Did the people who died on 9/11 live life abundantly? I thought about what had happened that day. I thought about the four men who were on Flight 11 that hit the north tower. Did they really honor their families when they took over the controls that fateful day? They said they were searching for justice. But where was the justice when almost three thousand people were killed? A question always burned in my soul: Did they demonstrate honor to their families, to God?

They were four men who seemingly led normal lives. One, Mohammed Atta, grew up like any normal Egyptian boy. His family and friends described him as a shy, unassuming young man who longed to make his position in the world known (Ezzat,

Ashraf, M.D. 2010). They said he must have undergone a stark personality change to become the terrorist who supervised September 11. He was the son of a lawyer and a homemaker. As a child, his interest was chess and he did not like violent games. He was a thin youth, only five foot seven.

As all fathers have a nickname for their child, his was "Bolbol," which was Arabic slang for a little singing bird. Atta seemed overpowered by his two sisters, who grew up to become a zoology professor and a medical doctor. Atta graduated from Cairo University with a degree in architectural engineering and was an average student, according to his peers (Cloud, John. 2001).

This quiet individual did not commit this evil act alone. The second hijacker was Abdul-Aziz Alomari. He came from 'Asir Province, a poor region in southwestern Saudi Arabia that borders Yemen, and graduated with honors from high school, attained a degree from the Imam Muhammad Ibn Saud Islamic University, and was married and had a daughter. However, he might have stolen another's identity. Even with that, where was the honor? Ah, two out of four, honor? Honor to his daughter and wife?

These men had partners in this evil crime. Waleed al-Shehri was the third hijacker. Studying to become a teacher like his brother, Waleed al-Shehri was also from 'Asir province. Since Shehri's family adhered to the Wahhabi school of Islam, he grew up in a very conservative household. His family did not have satellite television or Internet, and he was forbidden to play music or have contact with girls until he was old enough for an arranged marriage. An arranged marriage? Surely even his parents believed that to show honor, it was proper for parents to arrange a marriage. In stark contrast, a taping was supposedly found where he stated: "I am writing this with my full conscience and I am writing this in expectation of the end, which is near ... God praise everybody who trained and helped me, namely the leader Sheikh Osama Bin Laden."

How could anyone say that God praised this evil act?

One more man completed the ring of terror. His name was Satam al- Suqami. He had studied law in the local King Saud University. It is said that his passport was found on the day of September 11, 2001. He believed in honor, he studied law, and yet honor was overshadowed by evil. It is so hard to not focus on honor. Honor is a symbol that one is worthy of respect and admiration.

When God has specifically spoken by his inerrant Word, do we just turn away? As I walked to the university, I was reminded of God's Word. A long time ago in Sunday school at Saint Nicolas Eastern Orthodox Church, I learned what is said in 1 Peter 1:5–7, that we who believe in God are being guarded through our faith for a salvation that will be revealed in the last days.

However, we are continuously grieved by trials. These trials test our earnestness to be faithful. In Sunday school, I was taught that this faith is more precious than gold. Like gold, we go through the fire and are tested. We are tested daily, sometimes hourly or by the minute. But we are blessed because on the day of revelation, our efforts will be noticed.

*How, Lord, how can I continue to have faith when all around me I see hatred, especially from people who represent what I dearly love, my ethnicity?* I was so deep in thought that I didn't hear Jason calling my name.

"Doc! Hey, Dr. Santrew? Can I talk to you for a minute?"

I slowed down. "Sure Jason. I always have a minute for a questioning mind." I smiled. Sometimes Jason asked me questions that I had no answers for, and sometimes I thought he realized that.

"I have been thinking," Jason began. "I want to help somehow the women in the Middle East. Where can I begin?"

I looked at Jason, truly looked. He was so earnest and sincere. I could see how honor killing had hit his soul. I had to think a minute. Yes, there was.

"Jason, there is. It was just started this year. It is called OWFI. It stands for the Organization for Women's Freedom in Iraq. While this organization is focused with Iraqi women, they help women throughout the Middle East."

Jason smiled. "Well, Doc, thanks. I will look into it. See you in class." As he strolled away, he was starting to understand what I felt in my soul.

My deep roots were grounded in the symbolism of honor. I was raised to think that you take pride in all members of your family and what they have accomplished. You uphold honor by showing respect to family, extended family, and every person you journey through life with, as some may come and some may go. You honor God when you are humble and loving toward your family. When something happens that is not honorable, God bestows a correction in the journey of life. Honor is everything. Yet it is nothing. Today the world seems so void for feeling.

Tears came to my eyes. *When did we stop feeling as humans? When did we stop caring for our neighbors? If I had a child, would I truly want him or her to journey through life in the world that we live in now?*

The trudging through life consumed me. I was eaten up with the thought of how cruel this world is. Maybe tomorrow I could change the hole in my soul. But on this day, I felt void of feeling, drained. *Lord, help me to help others today. Let me honor your name and what you do in my life.*

As I turned, I saw that little girl again. I had seen her too many times. What was she trying to tell me? I needed to pray about this little girl. She was beckoning me, but why? I remembered that day's devotion by Charles Spurgeon, which said,

> A prayerless soul is a Christless soul. Prayer is the lisping of the believing infant, the shout of the fighting believer, the requiem of the dying saint falling asleep in Jesus. It is the breath, the

watchword, the comfort, the strength, the honor
of a Christian.

Was that little girl my watchword? Was she the child I never
could have?

# MOVING DAY OR
# MOURNING DAY

I couldn't believe we were moving. I was oh so sad. This was not supposed to happen. I was to grow up with John and David. I was supposed to go to college with them. And Lizbeth? Yes, even Lizbeth. Although sometimes she was too grown-up for me, she was like my big sister too. We were never supposed to be separated, and now look what had happened.

I thought back to the last day of school when I had to say my good-byes to my classmates. That was so hard to do. I had to say good-bye to my favorite teacher, too, and I couldn't stop crying.

It was the last week of school. Everyone was so quiet in homeroom. I had just come in from outside. I opened the door, knowing that I would never see my classmates again. The worst part of all was that I had to say good-bye to Mr. Ominetti.

Mr. Ominetti was my science teacher as well as my homeroom teacher. Because I was in a gifted school, I had had Mr. Ominetti for three years since sixth grade. He had taught me so much. I never liked science really, but he ignited the dormant fire of science within me. He allowed me to give science my best. And because of him, I did.

I will never forget him. Our relationship was deeper than that of a teacher and a student. He taught me a life lesson, perhaps the hard way. I will never forget the day that he unveiled my sin: the sin of smoking.

I always bought cigarettes at Daisy's, the neighborhood store. I don't know how she was able to sell them to me, but she did. I bought L&M's in the small red pack, small enough to hide them wherever I could. I used to hide them in a stoop of a real pretty brownstone across the street from the school. I knew I was too young to smoke, but everyone was smoking. Or so I thought. But I never wanted a grown-up to see me with them.

But I took them to school that year. One day, Mr. Ominetti asked me if I wanted to get out of math. He said that he needed help with setting up fifth period science lab. I was so happy that I didn't have to sit in Mrs. Antonelli's class, so I agreed and told him that I would be there for fourth period, which was right before lunch. I thought I would then already know what we were doing in science for that day.

When fourth period came, I handed Mrs. Antonelli the note from Mr. Ominetti. She looked a little out of sorts, but that was okay. I didn't mind. "Go ahead and go, Miss Handee. But make sure you do the homework for tonight, all right?"

I smiled. "Yes, ma'am, I certainly will." I was so happy. It was not that I thought Mrs. Antonelli was a bad teacher. In fact, she was great at teaching. I just didn't particularly like math that much. For the life of me, I couldn't understand how X times Y equals Q. Oh well. I knew that I wouldn't have to be concerned about those algebraic expressions when I grew up.

I went to Mr.Ominetti's class and opened the door gently. There were seventh grade students in the class at that time.

"Hi, Mr. O. Mrs. Antonelli said it would be okay as long as I did her homework."

He smiled. Something was up, I could tell. "Okay Michie. Give me a minute, and I will show you what I want you to do in the lab." I nodded and went into the lab to wait for him.

A few minutes later, Mr. O walked in with a smile wider than before on his face. "Michie, I found these today." He laid before me my pack of L&M cigarettes.

I knew right then I was caught. I could feel the color draining from my face. What was I going to do?

"Michie, I have decided to call your parents."

Mr. O rat me out? This couldn't be happening to me. I was a good girl, a good student, and very respectful. Little did I know that I was not respecting my body, a temple of the Holy Spirit. "You can't do that, Mr. O. I will get into so much trouble that I won't be able to see my friends or my cousins for a lifetime!"

I thought Mr. O was cool until now. "Well then, Michie, there is only one thing left to do."

*What was that?* I thought. *Throw myself into a burning fire across from the school?* That seemed easier than facing Mom and Dad.

Mr. O waited to respond. This was driving me crazy. Whatever he wanted me to do, I was ready to do it and hopefully survive my mom and dad's anger and disappointment.

"I want you to smoke the cigarettes." He smiled.

That was not a problem. One cigarette I welcomed. But he said "cigarettes," plural. "Mr. O, you want me to smoke a cigarette?"

Mr. O responded very firmly, "No, the whole pack."

*He has to be kidding. I will get cancer if I smoke one right after the other.* But the thought of Mom's and Dad's face when they received the call made me softly say, "Okay."

I proceeded to light and smoke one cigarette after the other. I could feel my stomach start to churn with nausea, and I was only halfway through the pack. Then I began to feel quite sick. "Mr. O, I can't smoke one more cigarette." I had already smoked fourteen.

"Well, Michie, I guess you will just have to smoke this." He put his hands in his jacket pocket and pulled out a stogy. The cigar had a red label on it that said "La Mira Handmade Cigar." It had been made in Cuba, which meant that it was expensive.

"Mr. O, isn't that a very expensive cigar?"

He smiled. "I think I can afford to help you with your smoking. Here, I will even light it for you."

I must have taken four puffs when I started to feel very, very sick. "I have to go to the restroom. I am going to be sick." I ran out the door, never so sick in all my life. After throwing up what I thought were my whole insides, I looked at my face in the mirror. I was as a white as a cotton ball. I made a promise to myself never to smoke again.

When I went back to the lab room, Mr. O was sitting there, smiling. "Michie, you had to be taught a lesson. You may be a tween, but you don't know it all. Cigarette smoking at your age could very well stunt your growth for your teenage years. I won't call your parents. But you have to promise me one thing, okay?" I nodded, too sick to even speak. "I want you to promise me that you will take care of yourself, both inside and out. That means that you will do appropriate-age things and not think about poisoning your body anymore. Deal?"

I started to cry. I don't know if the tears were because he really cared about me or because I was so sick. Either way, I learned a valuable lesson that day. My body is indeed the temple of the Holy Spirit. I promised myself I would keep that lesson forever in my heart.

Now, the last week of school, I was saddened. As I slowly pulled open the door, I thought to myself, *Science class is never quiet. What is going on? I hope not a smoking party again.* I had learned my lesson well from my encounter with the Cuban cigar. When the door was fully opened, suddenly I heard, "Surprise!"

The whole eighth grade was there, students in gifted and those in regular class, my other friends. Actually the whole eighth grade was a circle of all of my friends. Cynthia walked up to me and said, "We can't let you go without throwing you a good-bye party. I am for sure going to miss, my best friend." And with that, she started to cry. That was okay because I was crying too. I loved my life. Why did I have to leave it? My crying was interrupted by many hugs and good-byes.

"Michie, we have something special for you," Mr. O said. His eyes were glistening too. Scott came in carrying a basket of books. They all knew that I loved to read. Every time I walked down the halls, if I wasn't talking and socializing with my friends, I was reading a book. I know that seems hard to do. Actually, I had the reputation of bumping into people at their lockers because I was so into the story I was reading.

Brian came in next carrying a big pink stuffed toy. It was almost as big as me. On it were the signatures of the whole eighth grade. Over seventy of them.

"Thank you so much for loving me and letting me know how much you care." I could hardly talk from my voice breaking up. "I will never forget any of you. Whenever you are in Florida, please come by and see me. School is not going to be the same without you."

We ate pizza, sang songs, and laughed and cried. Yes, it was a good ending to a good life.

Now, I would have to move to a new state where the only one I knew was my cousin Masia. She was older than me, close to Lizbeth's age. She was a cool cousin. She was a majorette at her high school. *Well,* I thought, *maybe I can do some of the things that she does when I get to that godforsaken place called Miami. I guess that is something to look forward to.*

The week went by quickly, and despite the sadness I felt, I had the best week of my life in school with friends.

On a Saturday, when summer had officially begun, Dad was loading up the last small items into our station wagon. The movers had come the previous day. Now all we had to do was say good-bye to the family. My heart was so broken. I couldn't imagine a life without John, David, and Lizbeth.

Dad came in from the car. He looked at me, knowing that I was uncertain about this new journey. "Squirt, it is time to go." Aunt Salima and Uncle Paulie were outside our brownstone as well as my cousins. I couldn't stand this. I thought I had cried my last tear an hour ago and there I was, sobbing again. I gave everyone a hug, told them I would write often, and that maybe we could visit once or twice or maybe *fifty* times a year! That was highly unlikely, though. I hoped that maybe God would see to it that we could come back in a year. There was always room for dreaming.

I saw John and David sitting on the stoop. They were crying. We didn't know life without each other. They were like my brothers. We had shared so much. Even when I had the mumps John made it a fun time. He had designed a system with a flowerpot that had a rope attached to it. The system allowed us to write notes to one another. He would send me a note in the flowerpot, using the rope to navigate it to my window next to the fire escape. For ten days we did this, back and forth. Now, as I said goodbye, I didn't know if I could go on living. Tears like shattered glass ran down my cheek.

This was it. I was saying good-bye to my best friends. We kissed and hugged each other. Then John got up, gave me one last hug, and walked into our much-lived-in and loved brownstone. But David still sat, crying, not wanting us to go.

"Squirt, it's time to go."

I got into the car. I felt that the glass tears were now permanently etched into my face. As we drove off, I looked back. There was David, waving good-bye from the middle of the street. Yes, it was a sad, sad day. I didn't think I would ever get over it.

# HOME IS WHERE THE HEART IS

As I grew older, I knew that my heart was in New York. But after high school, I decided to join the army. Of course, Dad put his foot down and said, "No squirt of mine will do that. Besides, Michie, no offense, but you are a peanut. You are a princess. Princesses don't go off and fight battles. The battle belongs to the Lord. He will take care of it."

No matter how old I was, I always respected my parents' thoughts and feelings. I honored Dad by not joining the service. But I did decide to go back to the place I knew as my home, New York. Aunt Salima had room at her house, so she invited me to stay with her.

I attended Saint John's University, with Dad's blessing. This was where he worked after the service and was proud that I was accepted. While my parents were saddened that I had chosen to leave Miami, they were glad that I was going where I had family. Where there is a home, there is love, and that is exactly how I felt about Aunt Salima's house. I was fortunate to have two homes.

# A Trickle of a Dream

Kevin was not due home for at least two hours. An ominous feeling came over me. *Why when I am so happy, I feel confused and down? I have a wonderful marriage, great family, and a wonderful career. I have met my game. But what lingers like a haunt in the night?*

I looked out the window. Darkness had settled in the sky. I glanced at the lamppost, and like an old friend, the little girl was standing there again. I cried out, "Lord, what does her existence mean?"

I kept thinking that she was trying to tell me something. But what? My thoughts wandered to Jason. *Ah, Jason, you have pricked my heart with your undying enthusiasm. How can I help you understand the ways of a culture that sometimes are not my ways? I do not agree with the way things were handled. I do not approve that 9/11 killed so many people. It breaks my heart that dignity and lives were taken by people who come from a culture I love.*

The phone was ringing violently off the hook. "Hello?" My sweet prince was on the phone.

"Hey, Michie. I am near Atlantic Avenue. Do you want me to pick up some zata or meatpies?" That was my man. Always thinking of me. He really did love me, even when I was not lovable.

"Sure, hon. That would be great. I haven't eaten yet."

I heard him laugh. "Okay. See you in a little bit." His love refreshed my spirit and his laughter put a smile on my face.

It took him many years to eat our "Syrian pizza." He was not accustomed to having what he called sand on his pizza. Actually, it was not sand at all. Zahtar has an essence of spices to it. The pizza starts out with unleavened bread, and you spread a layer of olive oil on it. The sand, as Kevin called it, was made up of marjoram, ground sesame, oregano, sumac, and sometimes hyssop. It was delightfully tasty and one of my favorites. Kevin did not like it for a long time, but he grew to enjoy it as much as me. Yes, he had grown accustomed to my ways.

I, too, had grown accustomed to his ways. Two different worlds collided when we became one. I never knew what life was without love, and Kevin never knew what life was *with* love. He had gone through so much. He always said that he couldn't wait for the day when we had children. Unfortunately, that had not come to be.

My heart ached that we did not have children. I had prayed, begged, and even bargained with our Lord. Yet the quiver of our family remained empty. I looked at Suzie and saw how happy she was. So many quivers in her nest and still she maintained all that I did. She was a beautiful person inside. A new baby can always put more life into a person. She had a beautiful husband and a terrific position at the university. I was happy for her, yet a little envious. Why, though? Was it the children she had and I did not?

My mind traveled back to Jason. His enthusiasm made me wonder, just a little. Perhaps, just perhaps, there was a child in Iraq or Syria that needed a … No, I couldn't think about that. I didn't think Kevin and I could love a child that wasn't our own. Or could we? *"Stop, Michie,"* a little voice inside me says. *"This is a silly thought. You and Kevin have never even talked about it."* But for some reason, my heart was fluttering.

I walked to the window again and deliberately looked at the lamppost, but there was no little girl. I thought my mind was doing double time. I was letting my thoughts get the best of me. Suddenly, I remembered what Keith said when we were together. Ah, Keith. I never loved him like I loved Kevin.

# LOVE, SO SHALLOW, SO FUTILE

After my diagnosis of endometriosis, Keith was relieved. Everything was going so well until that day.

The following weekend was Joyella's wedding, and it was beautiful. The church had glistening, shimmery bows alongside each pew. I had chosen my dress especially for Keith. As I walked down the aisle with him by my side, I imagined that our wedding would be beautiful. The bows brought a fairytale feeling to the wedding.

When Joyella came into the church, she did not have a bouquet. As she walked down the aisle, each woman she passed handed her a pink calla lily. Each flower represented the woman who was special in her life. By the time she got to the altar, she had her bridal bouquet. What a blessed bouquet. It held so much love, respect, and gratitude for the lessons she had learned from childhood to now.

I whispered to Keith that I wanted roses that were dipped in gold, not real gold, but the illusion of real gold. He smiled, but he was distant. At the time I did not know why. I just thought that he was thinking about his upcoming art show.

The service was beautiful. The soloist sang "Evergreen" by Barbara Streisand. I had tears of joy in my eyes for Joyella. But when I turned to Keith, all I saw was a look of foreboding on his face. Something was up, but I, in my naiveté, did not know what.

After the ceremony, when Joyella and Jim came down the aisle, they stopped at every pew and thanked everyone for coming.

That certainly was original. I said to Keith "Maybe one day we can do this." Again, he smiled as if I were miles away. I shrugged. I was going to have fun no matter what.

The last to leave the inside of the church was Joyella and Jim, the new Mr. and Mrs. Brown. Kaleidoscopes of monarch butterflies were released, and the colors were beautiful. I made a note to myself that day.

After the ceremony, we went to the gala reception at Joyella's mother's house. They had positioned twinkling lights along the walkway with, again, glistening bows. As we walked in, we were greeted with an array of hor d'oeuvres that ranged from caviar to Oysters Rockefeller. The music was soft and romantic. We feasted that day and had a wonderful time dancing.

At the end of the reception, much to our surprise, a hot air balloon was set up in the outer garden of the festivities. Jim and Joyella mounted the air balloon and bid farewell to all. They were to land five miles from the reception where a limousine was to whisk them off to the airport for Bora Bora. What a romantic day!

But that sense of romance immediately ended as we got into the car. Keith was quiet. I turned and asked him, "Sweetie, where are we off to?" He didn't turn toward me. Looking straight ahead, he said in a serious manner, "I am taking you home. I have an appointment."

What? I couldn't believe this. We had just left a wedding, my *best friend's* wedding, and he was taking me home? I was so upset. I thought my world was crashing in. He was the love of my life. The one who had my total self entwined with his soul. How could he do such a thing? I asked him, "Why today of all days?"

"Michie, I had to schedule it. Sorry."

When we arrived at my house, he kissed me as if he were kissing me for the last time. "I will talk to you tonight or soon."

Tonight or soon? Was he kidding? Something was desperately wrong, and I had no idea what or why.

Later, I would find out all too well.

# THE LOSS OF FIRST LOVE

I drove to the Bayshore Club, a private club where we all hung out. Most of the patrons were into the arts and boating. I thought that I could drown my sorrows without anyone knowing. How wrong I was!

I went to the bar and sat down. My friend Tom was there, but we didn't really talk about anything special. I explained as simply as I could why Keith was not with me. He seemed to understand more than I was saying. We ordered something to nibble on. Tom was a good friend, someone I had always trusted.

When the food came, we were talking about prospective internships coming up. Suddenly Tom said, "Michie, let's go sit over there in the back." I asked him why when we had perfectly good seats. Tom was irritated, and I didn't understand why, until I turned around and there before me was the love of my life with another woman. Shocked and frozen, I didn't know how to respond.

Keith looked at me. "Michie, I told you—"

"You told me what, Keith? That you had an appointment? Well, aren't you going to introduce me to this very important person who you have a very important date with?"

As Keith turned to do this, all I could think of was to say, "You know, it is better this way. I have spent more time on this journey. It is time someone else cleaned the dirt off his feet. Good luck!"

Tom gently took my elbow and escorted me out. When we were outside, sobs came like wind breaking through trees in a storm. My heart felt shattered. I couldn't breathe. All Tom could do was hold me. "Shh, Michie. It will be okay. He doesn't deserve you. You deserve so much more."

I looked up at my dear friend. He was right. For three years, I had catered to Keith. I had given him my heart and soul, and now it was just ripped away. I told Tom, "I am leaving. This is too much for me." Tom kissed my forehead as if he were my big brother.

As I drove home, I thought of 1 Corinthians 13. "Love is patient, love is kind." Keith was not patient, and sometimes, like this evening, he was not kind. He was a hurtful, self-centered man. *Love does not envy, love does not boast. Love is not proud,* I thought through the tears that flowed from my eyes and the knife in my heart. Keith envied anyone who could do something better than him. He always imitated people and was quite condescending. He did not follow me like a man who thirsts for water as in a desert.

Love does not dishonor others. Keith did not honor me, not ever. How could he have put the knife in my heart and twisted it? "Love is not self-seeking, Love is not easily angered, Love keeps no record of wrongs." Every time I did something that Keith disagreed with, he kept a record in his mind and repeatedly reminded me of it. "Love does not delight in evil but rejoices with the truth." The truth? What did Keith know about truth in loving? By lying to me, being deceitful? "Love always protects, always trusts, always hopes, always perseveres." How could I have fallen in love with someone who was so untrustworthy?

As I drove through the rain pouring down my cheeks, I prayed that either the Lord would change my heart and take away the deep love I had for Keith or change Keith's heart. But I did not see that the Lord would change his heart anytime soon. I was so deeply hurt that it would take a lifetime of rights to change this wrong.

When the phone rang and I saw Keith's number, I did not answer it. As I entered my house, the phone rang again. It was Keith's brother, Ryan. "Hello?" I answered cautiously.

"Hey there, little sister. What is going on? I mean, Keith said you were done, finished, I—"

I interrupted him before he could hear my incredulous sobs. "Ryan, I don't want to talk about it. I love you. I always will. But Keith has taken my heart and drained every emotion out of me."

There was silence. Then as if on cue, Ryan said, "You know, Michie, he is not worthy of your love. He is shallow, always has been. The notches on his belt he hangs with honors. I am sorry, little sister. I should have told you a long time ago."

I thanked him. "I will keep in touch, Ryan. I doubt if I will ever hear from Keith again." We ended the call on a "love you forever" note.

As I laid my head on my pillow that night, I thought to myself, *Someday long after this hurt has healed, if it ever does, I will find my prince. The one who will hold the key to my heart forever. No matter what the circumstance, God knows who he is.*

# MY PRINCE, MY
# SOUL MATE

Yes, Kevin came into my life. At first I didn't know what to think of him. He was in my chemistry class, a class I hated, but I had to take it because it was a prerequisite. I remember the day clearly. I walked into the lab and saw this guy with mega muscles and long hair. Handsome, but not my type. I found out that he was a chemistry major, so I knew that if I had a chance, I might have him as my friend. For sure I could pass then.

Like a clock that never stops, the days ticked by, and we became friends. Kevin helped me through the assignments, and every day I liked him more and more.

The final test day came. I could tell that Kevin was thinking of something beyond the test. "You know, Michie. You are going to ace the test." I looked at him, smiling. "If I do it is only because of your tutoring me." As we walked into the lab, he said, "We'll see, future teacher. We'll see."

The test was anything but easy. I calmed my breathing as I attacked each question. My heart was palpitating. I didn't know if I was putting the correct answers down or not. When I finished the test, I waited for Kevin. Why was it taking him longer than me?

When he came outside, I had tears in my eyes. Kevin had a brain that could photograph the answers and remain in his thoughts. "Michie, I finished a long time ago. I was waiting for you. Don't panic. I am sure you passed. We will know in an hour. How about that coffee now?" He hugged me. He always reassured me. That hug was all I needed. I felt secure in it. It was so brief but long lasting. He gave me the confidence I needed.

An hour passed, and we went back to the lab. I was quite a bit calmer all due to Kevin. I looked up my student number. I passed? I passed! I jumped up and down.

All Kevin could do was laugh. "Michie, you know what I like about you?" I looked at him. "The way your curls are around your forehead. You nut, I told you. I knew you would pass." He smiled. "Did I tell you I love those curls around your forehead?" From then on, he was my prince. My soul mate. Never mind that there were times I drove him crazy. As we became a couple, I loved everything about him. His honesty was the greatest factor and his faith. That was the beginning of our love story, and it has never stopped. He asked me to marry him on my twenty-first birthday. I couldn't believe how he did it.

He had planned it so secretly and romantically. First, we ate at Convivium Osteria, a quaint Italian dinner in the heart of Brooklyn. It was located at 68 Fifth Avenue between Begen and Saint Marks. The three dining rooms transported you from a farmhouse in the Italian countryside where Carlo, the owner, was from, to a bodega in Barcelona, and lastly to a wine cellar in Oporto. In the first dining room, we had appetizers. That in itself was a dinner.

The second dining room consisted of our entrée. We loved it. We feasted on a wonderful dinner of filete de pagel con alcaparras, tomate, olivas y espinaca, which is red snapper fillet with capers, fresh tomatoes, olives, and spinach. Conviviium Osteria combines the Old World culinary and aesthetic traditions of Italy with a nod to Spain and Portugal. The finale was an Italian wedding cake, which I felt led me to gain at least five pounds. It was so delicious!

When Kevin first met me, he thought I was Italian, so naturally he sought out the best Italian restaurant in Brooklyn. This was where our first real date took place. Kevin knew that I loved this restaurant. The ambience took us places I had always dreamed of, and the candle on the table illuminated Kevin's beautiful face. I thought to myself, *How very much in love I am with this man. He holds me in his palm.*

After a festive dinner, we crossed the Brooklyn Bridge and drove to Central Park. Kevin had a reservation with a white horse-drawn carriage. It was a beautiful night. The stars sparkled like diamonds across a sea of serenity. Kevin had the carriage stop in front of a beautiful fountain with blue water flowing through it.

Gracefully, he extended his hand to me. We walked in silence, knowing that we didn't have to speak a word. In front of the fountain, Kevin got down on one knee and said, "Michie, I don't know what tomorrow may bring, but I do know that I don't want to spend my tomorrows without you. You are the girl I dreamed about when I was seven. A girl with brown hair with curls on her forehead and a heart for love. Will you be my wife and spend my tomorrows with me until they become my yesterdays and we sit on a swing sixty years from now?"

I had tears of joy in my eyes. "Yes, yes, I will be there as your wife. But no more chemistry classes, okay?"

He stood and hugged me for a tender moment, a moment emblazoned on our hearts forever.

# DREAMS ARE MADE
# OF GOLD ROSES

Our wedding day was November 27. The day was bright with the sun smiling down on us.

Much preparation had gone into the wedding. The night before was sparkling with excitement as we gathered for our rehearsal at the Brooklyn Community Christian Church. I had fallen in love with that church. Its mission statement was "Equipping godly men and godly women to build godly families and raise godly children." It was based on Psalm 78:4: "We will not hide them from their children, but tell to the coming generation the glorious deeds of the Lord and his might, and the wonders that he has done."

Our rehearsal dinner was at Palo Santo on Union Street. It was Ideal. The restaurant was tucked into the ground floor of a Park Slope brownstone. There were forty family members present. The night was brilliantly lit with love abounding for the coming day. Kevin and I were like two giddy children, curious for what God had in store for us.

Kevin presented his best man, his brother Chuck, with a beautiful wooden box made out of cedar. He chose this because the cedar tree had been revered for its spiritual significance for thousands of years. Its wood has been used for the doors of sacred temples and burned in cleansing ceremonies for purification. He wanted Chuck to know that their brotherhood was pure in spirit and deep or high in love and understanding. Kevin had it engraved with "It doesn't matter where you go in life … It's who you have beside you. Thank you for being beside me, especially now. " I loved that he cared for his brother so much.

I couldn't have my sister, Silvie, as my maid of honor. She was seven months pregnant and the doctor said that she couldn't travel. She still lived in Mississippi. Our love for each other was deep as sisters, so I knew that if she could have come, she would have. So I asked my cousin who was like a sister to me, Martha. She was a stunning beauty. Her olive skin looked so beautiful against the emerald dress she wore. More importantly, she was my rock and my mentor. She had been beside me emotionally and spiritually from the time I was a teenager.

I presented her with an alabaster box. In biblical terms, an alabaster box holds precious oil saved for something important. I had engraved on the inside, "When I walk down the aisle on the day I say, 'I do,' I'll put my flowers in your hands and I'll be proud to stand next to you. You'll be the one who is by my side on this very special day. You'll hold my strength in your heart because you stand for me in so many ways. You have walked with me many times before, and I am blessed to have you here now. I treasure the honor of having you by my side on the day that I say my vows. Martha, this is not only a symbol but also a statement of loyalty and trust. It gives new meaning to the bond and devotion we have between us." After she read it, we hugged, knowing that the new journey would separate us in distance but not by ties. We would journey through life together. We knew that no matter what stood before us, we would always be there for each other, especially at that moment.

Our wedding was shining with God's abundant love and grace. I wore a champagne dress with sequins, and my flowers were of roses dipped in gold! We had a unity candle, the lighting of which symbolizes the union of two hearts and lives. There were two taper candles placed on either side of the large pillar candle, or unity candle. The taper candles represented the lives of Kevin and mine as individuals prior to our union in marriage. Together we picked up our individual candles and in unison lit the center unity candle. We then blew out our own candles, symbolizing the end of our separate lives.

The candles signified the joining of two families into one. At the end of the ceremony my mom and Kevin's aunt Beatrice lit another candle, which signified the union of our two families. My love for Kevin and his love for me became one as we started our journey as man and wife with our Lord leading us.

As the sun set and the moon rose, our reception was that of a fairy tale. We had a white horse-drawn carriage escort us to my aunt Agora's house in upstate New York, which was made out of stone from the 1930s. She had lanterns on either side of the walkway with white and pastel tulle surrounded by satin ribbons and bows. She always had gold chandeliers so they added to the beauty of the reception. At every seat, Kevin and I placed pictures of the people sitting there, marking their position in our lives during our growing-up years and into the present. It was breathtaking!

The song "Someday My Prince Will Come" was playing in the main reception room. The whole night was joyful. Toward the middle of the evening, we put on Middle Eastern music, which is the tradition at my family's weddings. I walked to the middle of the dance floor, and the music flowed as I danced for Kevin. It was a sacred moment, representing that this was the time I would give myself to my husband wholly and honestly. Yes, there had been one before him. God had convicted him to love me as a whole woman, and he had convicted me in my spirit that I belonged to Kevin alone now. While others watched, we were entranced with each other.

The time came for the daughter and father dance. But Dad was not there. My heart knew it would ache, for Daddy was in heaven. But I knew he looked down and was smiling. So Uncle Paulie stepped in for my dad. He was the perfect substitute. And yes, we danced, not to a Frank Sinatra song, but to the song "Daddy's Little Girl." Tears flowed from my eyes. Uncle Paulie knew what I was feeling. He knew that if Dad could not be there, he would honor me as a daughter, at least for the moment.

The evening ended with Kevin and me leaving in our horse-drawn carriage. The next day, we flew to Boston. It was a presidential year, and we wanted to embrace the freedom of our country and also to see the history of our nation come alive.

We had engulfed our moments into each other. God was a God of wonder and miracles. He gave me my prince to share my tomorrows and to look back on my yesterdays.

I thank God for Kevin every morning, every afternoon, and when we are together at night, we thank God for each other.

# THROUGH THE
# EYES OF WISDOM

Over the next couple of weeks, Jason and I talked quite a lot about helping the OWFI. Each time we talked, we came to the same conclusion. Seemingly, women's rights were virtually nonexistent in Iraq, at least not in the way they are in the United States.

As our discussions deepened, my heart echoed a familiar tune. Children in the Middle East have no childhood. Furthermore, they are in the midst of a senseless war, one without end. The war in the Middle East continued to emblazon my heart with the need to do something. Jason's heart equally was set on fire with wanting to help. We didn't know where to start.

*If only ... I can't think of if only.* If only I did not think day and night about children all over the Middle East, who were in situations they did not ask to be in. My heart was swallowed up by the oppression those children saw every day through their innocent eyes.

I came from a childhood of cherished memories, growing up looking through glasses that only saw good in everyone and not evil. How could those children be denied that? I realized that it happened in every segment of the world. But still my heart had a hole in it because of who I was and what I had become.

I was given a miracle of a loving family. These children did not even have the hope or miracle of thinking that their lives were secure for one minute. As Jason and I talked, I continued to feel the need to do something. And so did Jason. But what? How could we fill this void? I also thought of Rachel. Of her heart aching for those children back in Tukatal. We indeed needed to fill the void to helping, somehow, somewhere.

It was almost Christmas, and the winter had hit New York hard. There had been three severe snowstorms that had knocked out the power for days. I was late doing my Christmas shopping for Kevin and the family. This year, we had decided that instead of buying big gifts, we would buy small ones and decide upon a charity to help. It was Kevin's idea. He was such a generous man. He convinced my cousins and his family to go along with this idea. His random acts of kindness never ceased.

# HELPING WITH THE
# HEART OF JESUS

I remembered how the year before Kevin had helped a woman with the electrical wiring of her home. It was just about the same time of year. Again, we had a snowstorm, and power was, of course, suspended. We were sitting in church when a young couple sitting next to us were talking about an older woman, maybe about eighty-five years old, who did not have the money to rewire her home.

Kevin, being the jack and sometimes master of all trades, told the couple that he might be able to help. The couple said that the woman lived on their block. After church, Kevin turned to me and said, "Michie, I think I want to go to the woman's house, introduce myself, and see what I can do." Of course I agreed with him, but it was after all the dead cold of winter. He said, "That is all the more reason to go." I agreed, and so we set out that very afternoon to find her home.

When we knocked on her door and told her that we had heard she was having electrical problems and would like to help her, she looked at us skeptically. After we told her that we attended the Brooklyn Christian Community Church two miles away and had heard that she needed help, she relaxed.

Her name was Idalle Buelle Habib. She was a little lady, no taller than four foot five. Dripping wet, she must have weighed no more than ninety pounds. "That is very kind of you," she said. "I could not afford the cost of an electrician, and I am too embarrassed to ask for help."

We understood completely. Some people are laughing on the outside but crying on the inside. In this case, Idalle did not even have the strength to laugh. She asked us to sit down and have some tea with her. Tea was very sacred to her. She brought back a pot of tea and began to tell us about the sacrament of drinking tea with friends and family.

As we settled down to her hospitality, we took note of how cold it was in her house. Idalle explained to us that many times when she was growing up she was cold because her family could not buy warm clothes. Her family was part Italian and part Syrian. *What a combination!* I thought. *Here we are, and once again, I see the roots of my culture. Strong, no matter what comes a person's way.*

Idalle further explained that when she was a little girl she would watch the grown-ups drink *shay*, which was tea, or *kahwa*, which was coffee. She was told that drinking these showed guests the symbolism of hospitality and generosity.

"Actually, they drank it all day long." Idalle sighed. "I remember young boys often carried large trays of demitasse cups to the shopkeepers. Perhaps in hopes of working or better, or worse, yet, a contractual marriage, depending on how you viewed the contract." Idalle, Kevin, and I laughed together.

I asked her what town she was from. Her mind wandered as if looking back into many yesterdays. "I came from a town east of Damascus. It was called Adra. It is an industrial city now. But when I was a little girl, I would walk with my father to the sugar factory. I would bid him farewell until I saw him again in the afternoon." Tears welled deep in the ebony eyes of this old woman. I was tempted to ask her what was wrong or what went wrong when she continued to talk. "There was a time when girls were hurt badly in the sugar factory. My sister was one of them. Her name was Faridah. That name means 'matchless, precious pearl.' She was hurt so badly that it took the life out of her soul. She was never the same. Faridah was my twin sister."

Sadness overwhelmed the three of us as we drank our shay. I looked at Kevin with tears in my eyes. Again, I could not comprehend how people could be so cruel.

Kevin tried to change the subject. "I am so sorry. But God spared you, and now you are here." Idalle looked at Kevin and touched his hand lightly. "Yes, he did, and look. I have met you both, and you are giving me the gift of generosity. How can I ever repay you?"

"You can invite us over again and tell us how you arrived here in New York. But for now, I must attend to the wiring." Kevin stood and asked where the electrical box was.

Idalle stood up and asked him to follow her. He took inventory of the situation and said he would have to call a friend from church who was an electrician. "But, Idalle, I do not want you to worry. We will get it fixed for you." Kevin turned and winked at me, which was always our signal to one another that it was time to go.

Idalle said, "Ma'a salama مع السلامة then, hatta naltaqi thaniyatan (حتى ثانية نلتقي)" It means good-bye until we meet again." With that, she kissed our cheeks three times, one on the left, one on the right, and one on the left again.

Kevin was taken aback, but Idalle explained, "Only in close friendship do we kiss three times. It symbolizes that we are close." She walked us out. I knew we would visit her often. Kevin and I both felt like we had known and respected her all of our lives. A Teta, of sorts.

# Purer Than a Tear

"Daddy, you really need to hear this song. Come quickly."

Dad was outside cutting the lawn. It was getting ready to rain. "Squirt, I need to finish this."

I jumped up and down. "Please, Dad. It is the song just for you and me."

Dad cut the mower off. "Okay, Michie. I am a coming." Dad never got mad at me. He tried to look perturbed, but I saw the smile behind his thick-rimmed glasses. He walked into the house.

"Don't forget to take your shoes off. You know Mom gets upset when blades of grass are in the living room."

Dad sat down Indian style right there at the door. As he listened, tears started to well in his eyes.

The song touched my heart and I wanted Dad's heart to be touched too. "Listen, Daddy." The song was "The Men in My little Girl's Life" by Mike Douglas. It tells of a little girl, and as she grows up, she shares the tales of the boys in her life. The final journey is when she falls in love with her prince. "Daddy, oh, Daddy, will there ever be someone as handsome or as good as you in my life?"

He looked at me as we both listened. By the end of the song, both of our eyes were welling with tears.

"That is a beautiful song. One day we will dance to that when that special man comes. Or maybe we will dance to 'Daddy's Little Girl.' After all, you will always be my little girl, no matter how old you are, Squirt. But for now, I am the man in your life who loves you and you are my princess. I want you to dance by the light of the moon as you grow. Remember what I have always told you?"

I smiled. "Yes, Dad. I am purer than a tear."

Daddy hugged me. "You got it. Now, sweet princess, I need to finish the yard before your mom gets after me."

That was my dad, always taking time to see me through emotions whether they were good, bad, or indifferent. He was the first date in my life. In my heart of hearts, I thought, *No, there won't be someone as handsome or as gentle as my daddy, my Sarge.*

# MY HERO, MY
# SOUL, GONE

After we moved to Miami, Daddy became a calmer person. He would make the most serious person laugh. When things weren't perfect, he had a habit of saying, "Well, you know you did the best that you could." Every measure of my life was based on the encouragement of my dad.

Even when I wanted to move back to New York to go to school, Dad encouraged me. Mom, on the other hand, was quite upset that I wanted to leave her. She just didn't understand. My home was with my family and the culture of New York. Mom and Dad were of course my family, but I missed my cousins dearly. I wanted to go to college and be near them.

Eventually, Mom relented, especially when I told her that she would carry my heart in her heart. The flight from Miami to New York was only three hours. She came for a visit the first week of college and her mind was changed. That was when she met Kevin.

Kevin and I started out as friends. My mother looked at him for the first time and said to me, "Someday he'll be my son-in-law." I laughed because at that point Kevin was not my Prince Charming. The fact that we were just friends made our relationship more balanced, more fruitful. Besides, he was a whiz at science. I never thought that we would marry. But things changed over time.

About two months into Kevin's and my relationship, something happened to Dad that would not allow him and me to dance at my wedding. He was working at a construction site on a rainy day in Miami. He always hated to work in the rain. The winds were blowing strong. He had just one more board to place on the home he was building before they laid the stucco over it. Sam, his boss but more importantly his best friend, told him to get in from the rain. Dad, being a sound man but still stubborn, said he would finish in a jiffy. Just then, a gust of wind picked up. Dad was standing on a twelve-foot ladder. The wind came over him like a blanket, only one with an ulterior motive. The blanket of death could be felt.

Dad fell off the ladder and broke his leg. Sam heard the crash and came running over. He saw that Dad was in pain, and that his leg was turned backward like a pretzel. Sam tried to calm him down as the other workers called an ambulance. "Sam, Sam, if I have to live with this, I can't stand the pain! It is much worse than before!" Sam said, "Hey, Ole Sarge, none of that now! You are meaner than a two-headed billy goat. Ain't nothing going to happen to you. Besides, Michie needs you to walk her down the aisle. Remember that."

Dad looked at Sam with tears in his eyes. "I am tired, Sam. Tired of working and never seeing the light of peace." At that, the ambulance came.

They took Dad to the nearest hospital. His leg was beyond broke. He had broken all three bones in his right leg, the femur as well as the tibula. And so was dad's soul. The doctor assessed this fact.

Mom called me. "Michie, something has happened to Dad. He will be all right, though. He broke his leg, and they are going to operate in the morning. You don't have to come now. However, make reservations."

Dad hurt! My hero hurt! The pain of the past crept up like a fog on a starlit night. I couldn't have anything happen to Dad. He needed to be here with me. I wanted to protect him and Mom. Numb, I made the reservations, praying with all my heart that

God would watch over him. But I could not get a flight out due to the bad winter weather.

I called Mom and told her that I would arrive on Wednesday. She tried to assure me that everything was under control. "Mom, can I ask you to do something?"

"Michie, what kind of question is that? I will do whatever you ask. You are our little girl no matter how old you are! Now what is it?"

"I want you to tell Dad to hang on. Kiss him and tell him that, okay?" Mom agreed she would.

The next twenty-four hours were grueling. During that time, my cousin in Miami, Masia, called. "Michie, they are going to put your dad in a body cast. They say that it will be safer for him, as the leg is too broken. They may have to transfer him. The doctors said that this is the only way they could keep mobilization to a minimum."

"Masia, they can't put him in a body cast! They are made only for children twelve years and younger" Talk to the doctors!" She assured me she would.

*That's it,* I thought. *I am calling Dad.* I knew it would be hard for him to talk, but I had to hear my hero's voice. I quickly dialed his room. "Hello, Dad. It's me, Michie. How are you doing?"

I could hear the pain and tears in his voice. The pain of giving up. "I can't talk right now, Squirt. I am in too much pain."

"Okay, Daddy. I will see you tomorrow. You hang in there, okay?" With that, we hung up.

A little girl grows up to be a woman, but her hero remains. That is how it had always been for me. My dad, my hero. That night I prayed that the Lord would send angels to protect Dad until I could get there.

Around 4:45 a.m., I woke with a start. Usually, I could go right back to sleep, but something was tugging at my heart. My flight wasn't to leave the airport until 1:00 p.m. I knew my waking up had to do with Dad. *Please, Lord, protect Dad. Protect him from further hurt and pain. Keep him safe in your arms today.* I slowly felt myself doze off.

Again, I woke with a start. Someone was ringing the doorbell. It was my cousin David. David had rededicated his life to the Lord, yet he looked like he had been out on a drunken spree. "David, are you okay? What's wrong?"

He fell into my arms. "Michie, he is gone. Your dad is gone. He died a half hour ago."

I held onto David with so much strength. I cried, "Why, Lord? This couldn't have happened. Why?"

My hero was gone. My soul was so empty. How could I live life without Dad? He was always there for me. Even when he was in the service, I knew he would come home. I didn't even get to say good-bye. My heart was broken and so was my bridge to my dad. Gone too soon. Gone before he could walk me down the aisle. Gone before he could hold his grandchildren. Gone. Like the wind that initiated this fateful journey, he was gone. There was a solitary calmness in my heart. I knew that nothing could bring Dad back.

As I packed, I remembered the song I thought he and I would dance to. The song that Dad would never hear again. "The Men in My Little Girl's Life." No, he wanted "Daddy's Little Girl" played when we danced. Now there would be no dance with the first man in my life. That dream was gone forever.

I dropped the shirt I was folding and cried out, "Lord, why?" Tears flowed from my eyes. My dad was purer than any tear. He was purer than the sunshine of all my days to come. My hero was safe now in the arms of Jesus. But for me. the little girl that day so long ago, now had to face tears of new beginnings of joy, sadness, happiness, and isolation from the one person who had made her laugh no matter what the shadows of life brought. My dad.

# A TIME SUCH AS THIS

عُرِفَ السبب بطل العجب ذا "When the reason is known, there will be no more wonder." (This is said when you are wondering why something happened and then find out.)

It was a Saturday morning. The winter storms had passed, and Kevin and I were eating breakfast. "Kevin, I have decided something. I have prayed and prayed about what I am going to tell you. God has blessed this decision. Now I need your blessing."

Kevin searched my face for answers. "Michie, go on."

I explained to him that I felt the need to go to Syria. I felt that Jason and I could do so much good enabling women to be free, teaching them that there is more strength than they have if they have someone to facilitate that strength.

"Kevin, I saw a poster yesterday at the university." I slipped him a picture of the poster. There was a little girl on it, eating out of a box and living in a bigger box. The poster had on it: "I am a child without a shelter, without a homeland and this world is without a heart or compassion."

Kevin looked at the picture and then at me. "Sweetheart, if this is your desire and you have time off from the university, I can't stop you. I want you to be who you are and fulfill your goals. No, I don't want you to go. But I know you have to. All your life you have prepared for this. Go with Jason, spend the winter break there. See with your own eyes what is possible. You know with God everything is possible. You have my blessing. Just come home to me in two or three weeks. The bed will get awfully lonely without you. Besides, I need someone to make shay for my every now and then."

I ran to his side and embraced him. Kevin was the next hero in my life. I could do nothing, aspire to be nothing, or live out my dreams without him. He was truly my soul mate. "Honey, thank you, thank you! I am so excited and happy! Jason will be too."

I quickly cleaned the kitchen. The next task ahead was to call Jason. I dialed his phone number, shaking with anticipation. *Jason, pick up the phone!* On the third ring, when I was about to hang up, he answered. "Jason, pack your bags. Kevin said we could go to Syria. I have made arrangements with the OWFI in Iraq. They said that our contact will be Jospeh Messalem. He heads the SOS Children's Village near Aleppo in Syria." I couldn't contain myself. I was so happy. My dream of helping children in my culture was coming true.

"Hey, Prof. Slow down. I haven't even opened my second eye. Tell me what you are thinking."

I explained everything to Jason. I told him that I had the money to go for both of us. All I needed him to do was say yes. I asked if he had his passport ready. We talked a little while longer. I knew that we could get an emergency tourist visa.

"Okay, so we are a go for sure?" Jason was starting to sound as excited as I was. "I will get on the ball. Catch you later."

As I hung up, I wondered what this little miracle of blessings was filled with. I wondered why Jason and I thought we had the capability to make things happen. I didn't know what I was getting into, but I did know that God was in charge and I was to follow where he leads.

I looked out into the day. There she was, standing under the lamppost. *Why is she always there?* There is always a reason. I was about to find out why.

# A VISA FOR HOPE

I knew what we were up against. It was not safe by any means. Americans were not welcomed in that part of the world. Still, Jason and I had a mission. My thinking about actually moving forward on this wild trip with him was exhilarating, if for no other reason than a humanitarian one because in our heart of souls, this was what we were destined to do.

We were warned several times not to go into Aleppo. The embassy warned us that humanitarian workers needed special authorization to get there and that journalists and educators were not the exception. Those individuals could be captured or killed as well. I didn't know it when I first met Jason, but now I saw God's writing on the wall.

It seemed that Jason did have ties to Syria and the Middle Eastern culture. When he was quite little, he had a neighbor down the street from where he lived who had a son named Jay. Originally, Jay and his parents and sister had resided in Aleppo, Syria. Actually, his real name was Jaweeb. However, since they lived in America, his parents did not want him called Jaweeb outside of their home.

Jay was the same age as Jason. They were both nine years old at the time. They were inseparable. They were in the same class at school. They played baseball together at the local 4-H club and encouraged one another. When Jay had trouble with spelling and vocabulary, Jason mentored him. Likewise, when Jason had trouble with multiplication and division, Jay was his tutor.

One day, it had been raining really badly. The boys were anxious for school to finish so they could get in some throws before the baseball game, which was scheduled for 5:00 p.m. This was an important game. It would decide who would play the all-conference for the baseball midgies game.

After school, Jason and Jay sprinted across the basketball court. The baseball field was right behind the school, so their parents didn't mind that they went without them. It was only a short time before they would be there anyway.

When the boys arrived at the field, there were four or five other teammates throwing the ball to one another on the diamond and warming up. Suddenly, Alex, a tall, gangly boy, threw the ball so far that went right out of the park. Jay quickly raced across the field and ran right into the street. He never saw the truck that was coming.

As if in slow motion, Jay hit the ground. Jason was in shock. Alex grabbed him, and someone else yelled for the coach. Within seconds, although it seemed like a lifetime, the ambulance was there. But the impact of the hit and the fall was to prove the worst. Jay never regained consciousness.

Jay's parents were devastated. He was their only son. His dream of becoming a doctor and helping those back in Aleppo were shattered. More importantly, their heart birthed a hole that could never be filled. Nor would Jason's heart feel the same brotherhood with anyone else as he did with Jay.

Days became weeks, which turned into months and years. Jason vowed that if he ever had the opportunity to somehow avenge the death of his eternal best friend, he would. It wouldn't be a vengeful act but rather a humble humanitarian act for the remembrance of his childhood friend.

So there was our connection. Out of searching, Jason and I found the mission we had both been searching for. After all, we had ties that would not be broken.

The visa would take longer than we had anticipated. We were told that it would take two weeks for the visas to come through. I was just so excited that I didn't think we would have to wait. Finally, the day came when we received our visas. We quickly made our flight reservations. We were to leave January 15 and return February 18. The average temperature was a high of 55 degrees and a low of 39 degrees.

We weren't going to a ball, so that eliminated my thirty-some-odd pair of shoes. Kevin told me that it would be better to have a carry-on bag that didn't weigh over forty pounds. That way, if I had trouble when I transferring airlines, it would be easier. My commonsense man! How I adored him.

As the day drew nearer, Jason and I anticipated what would happen in Aleppo. Would we be able to have the opportunity to do some good? Would the Syrians in charge shut us out? I was determined to see that we would have our dream fulfilled. While we waited, we prepared our belongings. We packed lightly.

Kevin had given me the go-ahead, but I knew it was breaking his heart. He knew it was something that we had to do, that it was our goal, but we didn't know what the end result would be. Still, my man, my knight in shining armor, stood by me. He didn't understand why I had the desire to pursue this thing that kept my mind racing and unable to rest till the deed was accomplished. What deed remained to be seen. All that was evident was Jason's and my burning sense that God was calling us to be there. And Kevin stood by my irrational need to go without a purpose because the purpose was yet to be revealed. Kevin truly loved and supported me, no matter how crazy my ideas seemed to be.

After packing, I took the time to call Suzie, who was now ready to go back to work. I explained to her what was going on.

"Girl, you are loco en la cabasa (crazy in the head)! Okay, I will do it. But if you get kidnapped and killed, I am going to be very upset." With that, she said she loved me and that it would be no problem taking over the class.

Of course, I had to tell Dr. De Palma, who had known of my plight for many months. He gave me his blessing, along with warnings that were quite similar to Suzie's.

I knew that I was loved but more so that I was supported in what Jason and I were about to do.

# LEAVING MY PRINCE

The rain fell softly as I packed the last of my bags. Was I making the right decision to go into unchartered territory? At least in my mind it was unchartered. I knew that my plight was inevitable, but was it really what God wanted? Jason and I shared the same ideal. Women and children were being harmed under the auspices of political gain. It broke my heart each and every time I watched the news. My blood was filled with the love of being who I was and I knew that I had to stand up for that love.

Kevin was playing Phil Collins's "Against All Odds," which was the song of the moment. I was going to return to him. We were not fighting against all odds. I knew in my heart that he understood.

The doorbell rang. It was Jason. He was so excited about this venture. "Hey, Prof, I am ready to help those women and children! Are you?"

Yes, I was. More than anything in life, I knew what was in store, the fear, the excitement, the unknown. All of it consumed me. More importantly, I knew I had to find my reason to carry on for all the tomorrows to come. As I cried, I knew that everything that consumed me meant that this was my destination. Kevin would have me in his heart and I would have him in mine. He understood. Others could not trust my decision because they could not explain or understand it. But God did and he would reveal his decision in time, if not to Jason and me, then to others. Through bad times on that trip, Kevin's strong arms around me wold protect me, even if it was only a thought, a memory, a reminder of something to come back to. Kevin knew when destiny called me that I must be strong. He may not be with me but he said that I had to hold on with this decision. In time, people would see.

Kevin and Jason loaded the baggage. I looked once more at our beautiful abode. Nothing could make this permanent until I found out what my purpose was. I took one more glance at the corner. The little girl smiled and pointed to the sky. Why was she smiling? Perhaps her lineage lay in the path I was to embark on. Whatever lay in store, the reason would become clear.

# ONE LEG CLOSER

The weather was dreary as Kevin dropped us off at the airport. "Remember, just put your faith forward, Michie. You are good at that."

I hugged him as tight as I could, trying to encapsulate the moment when time would stand still. I didn't want to leave Kevin. Yet I knew I had to make this journey, or pilgrimage, some might think. I had to find out what this little girl meant. Who was she? Why, when in the deepest moments of thought, whether of good or bad, did she appear?

I looked into Kevin's blue eyes and knew without a shadow of a doubt that I was making the right choice. I kissed his cheek and then his lips, holding on to the kiss that would be my last memory until my return.

"Thank you for loving me all these years. You were the only gift from God that I ever needed and wanted."

Kevin smiled. "You, my dear, are my gift. You taught me how to love and how to understand that we need to pursue our desires, no matter where the journey takes us. We need to find the reason why. Michie, I love you."

And with that, he left. Jason and I stood at the terminal as I watched the prince of my life drive away. *What If I don't return? What if ...?* I was not going to let my mind wander. There before us lay the answer to all the questions I had had over the years. There before us lay the answer of that little girl. This thought became reality as we went through security and luggage check.

# HOW MUCH
# MORE, LORD?

We were flying Air France from New York to Dublin. The flight would take about six hours. As we boarded the plane, I thought to myself, *Dad would be so proud that I am going to Dublin.* He always wanted to go to the Emerald Isle. His heart was always Irish. From the time I was a little girl, he reminded me of that. "Danny Boy" was his favorite song, and he always sang it to me. The Emerald Isle—majestic and romantic. But Jason and I would be there only for a few hours before going to a place, Aleppo, Syria, that still held a question. Why did both of us have this place so heavy on our hearts?

We settled into our seats. It was 4:00 p.m. My head hurt from crying and saying good-bye to my gem, my husband and the light of my soul. I turned to Jason.

"Hey, Prof, don't even think twice. There is no turning back now. We are doing this journey to help others, right?"

I smiled. Jason, who at first was a thorn in my side, had become not only my student, my mentee, but also a good friend. A friend who had the same desire for justice for women who were persecuted all in the name of war and superiority amongst the men of their culture and inequality for women who, in most instances, did nothing but honor the men around them.

"No, Jason, 'it's too late, baby now, it's too late.' You know, just like the song by Carole King, right?"

He chuckled. "Yes, Prof, but please do me a favor. Do not sing. It really gives me a headache."

I laughed as I placed my chair back because we were in the air by now. "Okay, I get it. You give me a headache, but I can't give back atcha? I will, my dear student, rest my eyes on that one." As a closed my eyes, I knew that no sane person would think this was a good idea. Yet I had prayed and sought God about it and knew in my heart that I was going to save my tomorrows and understand my yesterdays. The answers would come, and I was one leg closer to finding them.

# "Danny Boy"

"Daddy, the luck of the Irish is here today and we are going to the parade. Yippee!!!"

Dad smiled his crooked smile and laughter came deep from within his belly. "Yes, Squirt, and it is almost time for us to head on over to Fifth Avenue. Make sure you put your green on or else everyone at the parade will be pinching you!"

I ran around the dining room table as Dad pretended to have a hard time catching me. Mom called from the bedroom, her voice stern but with a little laughter in it. "Michie, I have told you a hundred times not to run around the table. Jiddo and Teta will have a headache downstairs from the way you are running!"

Dad and I chuckled. Jiddo always got upset with us kids, but Teta, well, she was a special lady. She never got upset at her grandchildren. "Mom, it is Daddy, not me!"

I walked quietly to my bedroom to put on the green kettle-cloth dress Mom had sewn for me. It was a special day indeed. Masia, my cousin from Miami, had flown up with her school. She was leading her school orchestra as the head majorette. I was so proud of her. One day I wanted to lead a parade.

It was cold outside and rainy, but that never stopped the parade. In New York, parades went on unless there was sleet or snow. Today was special, no matter what.

Lizbeth, John, and David were coming with us. My three surrogate siblings. How I loved them! I don't know what life would have been like without them. *Cousins and sisters and brothers are all the same, no matter what*, I thought. I went to kiss my grandparents and said, "See you later." I never said good-bye because that meant I wouldn't see them again. I prayed to God every night that I would always have them around. I loved them so much. When Daddy was in Korea, they were always there for me when Mom had to work.

We all pushed into the Rambler. I thought we had better hurry or else there would be traffic on the Brooklyn Bridge and we wouldn't get to see Masia. Sure enough, the traffic had been building up. I prayed to God to please let the traffic go fast. Once again, God did as he had promised. "I will never leave you or forsake you." We were right on time, *and* he gave us a parking spot right off Fifth Avenue!

The rain was so cold. Poor Masia! She would get drenched. We all huddled together as Mom said to the five of us, "I will be right back. I want to give Masia this raincoat at least until she starts marching." I wanted to go with her to see the glamour of being a head majorette. But no such luck. Mom insisted that I stay with the others, and I respectfully obeyed. Plus Dad's gigantic hand was on my shoulder, warning me that I had better not try to go.

Mom was only gone a few minutes when the parade started. The bands were harmonious as we stood on our tiptoes to see it all, and Dad lifted me up onto his shoulders. Masia's school band came into view. John and David started jumping up and down as if any second they were going to explode with excitement. "There she is, there she is!"

There was Masia in a stunning march. Her majorette costume was green and white. The white tassels looked like those on an Indian headdress. The rest of the costume was green velvet. Just as she came close to us, the band was playing "Danny Boy" and a rainbow appeared high above in the sky. God knew just what to do. Daddy smiled and looked faraway as the words repeated in my mind:

> For I'll be here in sunshine or in shadow,
> Oh, Danny boy, oh Danny boy, I love you so.

That Irish verse that day etched itself on my heart.

Yes, that moment will always be in my heart. I don't ever want to forget my roots and who I belong to. I belong to Dad and Mom with my cousins by my side. More importantly, I belong to Jesus!

# CROSSING INTO
# UNPROMISED LANDS

It seemed like only a minute had passed when I opened my eyes. I must have really been tired. The captain of the plane told us to fasten our seatbelts for landing into Dublin Airport. I turned to Jason, who looked like his thoughts were a thousand miles away, probably still in New York.

"Jas, are you okay?"

He looked at me with glistening eyes. "Yeah, Prof. I was just thinking, what if we are not welcomed by the orphanage? What if we …?" He didn't finish his sentence, and I did not want him to.

"We are going to be fine, Jason. God has appointed us to take this journey together for a reason. I don't know what that reason is. Usually, we don't see God's hands in the things we do until after they are over. But I am here to tell you that this journey has been prayed for many, many times by friends and family all over the world. I need you to be strong when I am weak. I now am being strong because you are weak. We will be fine."

"Anything you say, Prof. Just remember one thing. I won't eat any grape leaves unless you cook them, okay?" We both laughed.

"Jason, do you remember when you first came to our home, you asked why I cook so much?" He nodded. That time was the first of many dinners together along with Kevin. "My answer to you was 'food is not merely sustenance of life, but a way of life. Syrian dinners bring together family and friends. Just as long as it takes to prepare these dishes is how long friendship takes. That is why I cook so much.'" Jason nodded again as we disembarked from the plane.

I felt renewed energy and confidence as we walked through the terminal. Our flight had taken a little over six hours, and now we had to get to the Delta Airlines terminal to catch our flight to Aleppo, Syria. We had originally booked on Syrian Air. However, with the conflict between Syria and Israel, Syrian Air had canceled flights from Ireland to Syria. Usually, these flights from Delta were overbooked. However, a week before our journey, we were able to secure two seats on Flight 1060 leaving at 5:00 a.m. As luck would have it, we would have to catch a shuttle to the terminal for Delta and, of course, go through customs again.

The shuttle was an enjoyably ten-minute ride to the terminal. "Danny Boy" was playing throughout the shuttle, which brought confirmation to our journey to Aleppo. Dad and Mom were watching over us, along with Jesus, confirming that we were doing the right thing. Still in my mind I wondered if we doing the right thing. Then in my heart of hearts came God's Word from a song, <u>Standing on the Promises,</u> I remembered as a child:

> Standing on the promises I cannot fall,
> Listening every moment to the Spirit's call
> Resting in my Savior as my all in all,
> Standing on the promises of God.

I had God's promise that he was there to bring us into the land of promises, or unpromises. "'For I know the plans I have for you,' says the Lord. "They are plans for good and not for disaster, to give you a future and a hope'" (Jeremiah 29:11).

# Unpromised or Promised, the Forge Continues

Flight 2816 to Aleppo, Syria, was on time. Jason and I found our seats quickly.

The plane was full. There were more men than women. I presumed that they were men who traveled regularly. There was, however, one little girl who caught my eye. She looked so much like the little girl who kept coming to me as an apparition. Her hair was long and silky. She kept it back with a hairband. Her eyes were innocent, yet they also showed wisdom beyond her years and held deep sadness. I imagined that if she was going home, it is where she rather not go. She seemed to be around seven years old. I wondered what she was thinking. Her posture was pensive, and she was silent.

The adult sitting beside her was a woman. She was Muslim, or so I thought, because she was wearing a thawb. On top of the thawb, she wore a black abaya, which symbolized her culture and modesty. It draped around her body and down to her ankles. She wore a beige hijab, which was the head covering. The woman had her eyes closed as if in deep prayer. I made a note in my mind to say hello after the pilot turned off the seatbelt sign.

As my thoughts returned to our flight, I glanced over at Jason. He was sound asleep. At the beginning, I wondered why Jason was so intent on understanding the Middle Eastern culture. However, as I grew to know him and his relationship with Jay, I grew to understand the bond of two boys who forged love for each other as brothers that would take them into eternity. Jason was doing this for Jay.

The flight was to be five hours and forty-six minutes to the Nejrab Airport in Aleppo, so we needed to rest while we could. Neither Jason nor I really knew what to expect. I had wondered if accomplishing this journey would give me the answer I was searching for. All my life, my heritage, after God, meant more to me than anything else. My God, my husband, and my family were top priority to me. They were the heartbeat of my soul.

As I looked at Jason, I was reminded of the Lebanese writer Kahlil Gibran, whose words rang in my heart: "It is well to give when asked, but it is better to give unasked, through understanding; and to the open-handed the search for one who shall receive is joy greater than giving." Jason, too, was giving me so much. It was his motivation and enthusiasm to visit the women and children of Aleppo that had brought us to this very moment. Jason had a heart for giving without asking for anything in return. How could I not feel motivated when there was someone who had the same questions I did?

I must have drifted off again. The pilot was saying that we were hitting some turbulence, so we had to make sure we had on our seatbelts. As I focused, I remembered about the little girl. I had to say hello. I don't know why, but I felt like God was pushing me toward her.

It was a good twenty minutes before the pilot turned off the seatbelt sign. Jason by now was fully awake. As I stood up, Jason asked, "Hey, Prof, where are you going?" I gave him the rundown of how the little girl had caught my eye and that I had the desire to introduce myself. "Prof, forgive me for asking, but do boys ever catch your eye?" He winked, letting me know that he was not serious.

"Jason, I will be right back." With that, I started down the aisle.

The little girl was playing with a Middle Eastern Barbie-type doll. I knelt in the aisle. When she turned toward me, it took me aback. She looked so much like the girl in my visions! "Hi there. How is your doll today?"

The little girl looked first at her mother and then at me. Her head tilted quizzically, wondering what I was saying. It was obvious that she did not speak English. The woman who sat next to her spoke. "As-salam alaykom! How are you?" A smile broadened her tan face. I smiled, glad that she did not rebuke me.

"I am fine, thank you. Your daughter looked so familiar that I had to come up and say hello. I hope you do not mind."

The woman put out her hand in a warm gesture. "Not at all. She is not my daughter. I am simply bringing her to Aleppo to meet with her family again. Shaima, say hello to …?"

Shaima in Arabic means "one who has beauty spots." And she was beautiful and so precious. I couldn't take my eyes off her. She waited.

"Hi, Shaima. My name is Michelle. I wanted to say hello to you. Your doll is very pretty."

The woman glanced at me again. "My name is Basmah. It is nice to make your acquaintance."

I smiled at Basmah, realizing that she must have thought I was crazy.

"Shaima, tell her about your doll. شيماء أقول لها عن دمية الخاص"
She spoke in Arabic so I had no clue as to what she was saying, hoping only that she was telling Shaima to tell me about her doll. Basmah translated her words to me.

"Michelle, this is Razanne. It is similar to your Barbie doll. The outfit she is wearing … Oh please, sit down." Basmah gestured for me to sit in the other seat on the aisle. How silly of me to be kneeling when all along there was an empty seat! "As I was saying, Shaima has her doll wearing an outfit appropriate for Eid Al Fitr holiday. This is the holiday that is a month-long fast for Ramadan. Before the Eid, the entire family goes out shopping for new clothes to wear for Eid Day. Early Eid morning, the family meets with other members of the community for an Eid Prayer and then disperses to family gatherings and other celebrations. This is the outfit that Shaima's mother gave her before last Ramadan for her doll."

I told Basmah that I thought Ramadan was a sobering holiday. Basmah laughed. "Well," she said, "it is, but this is the time that children are happy as well. Children are often given gifts of toys or money, and families exchange delectable sweets that differ according to the region in which they live. So that is why Razanne is wearing a brightly colored hijab and abaya. She will celebrate with her owner, Shaima."

Her eyes looked toward the floor. "Her parents were killed in Aleppo five months ago. Her aunt placed her in the orphanage because she could not care for her. Shaima became ill. I am a humanitarian nurse. When I saw Shaima, she was so, so frail. I convinced the orphanage that she needed medical help. They gave me thirty days under the agreement that I was to bring her back." Basmah covered Shaima's ears. While Shaima did not understand English, Basmah wanted to make sure that she did not hear anything. "I hate to bring her back, but in accordance with the government, I have to, otherwise my visa will be revoked and I will not be able to help the orphanage."

I smiled, trying to hide my shock. My hands were clammy, and I thought my heart would beat out of my chest. I put on my fake appearance so as not to show my shock. Was this what God was leading me to? Trying to make the conversation lighter, I said, "There is much to learn about Middle Eastern girls." I continued to explain that I, too, am Middle Eastern. However, I cautiously explained that I was also a Christian.

"I am as well," said Basmah. "I wear these clothes whenever I go back to my homeland out of respect for my parents. So tell me, what brings you to Aleppo?"

# THE JOURNEY OF
# TEN THOUSAND
# MILES BEGINS WITH
# ONE FLIGHT

I told Basmah to excuse me for one minute while I went to speak to Jason. The thoughts running through my head were going so fast. Shaima looked just like the little girl who kept coming to me in visions. How could this be possible? I felt like I was living in a transcendent dream. This couldn't be reality. Or was it? Was this God's promise?

I quickly explained to Jason what was occurring, and he smiled. "God is giving us miracles. Now go on, Prof. Find out all you can about the orphanage and Shaima. We still have two hours before we land. I, on the other hand, will rest my weary young bones."

I hurried back to Basmah and Shaima and sat down. For the next forty-five minutes, I explained to Basmah why Jason and I were going to Aleppo as well as my background and the visions I had had. She took in everything I was saying, looking pensive, not quite believing all of it. Meanwhile, Shaima had fallen asleep. She was so beautiful. Her brown skin was shining and her hair was draped over her shoulder as her head lay in Basmah's lap.

Finally, after I finished, Basmah took a deep breath. "I am awestruck with what you are telling me. As strange as it sounds, perhaps God has chosen us to take this flight together for reasons we do not readily know. Perhaps when you get settled in Aleppo you can come to the orphanage. I live there intermittently when I am not taking children back and forth."

I straightened up in my seat. "Basmah, we are both Christians. I don't know all the ways of our Lord, but I do know that his words tell us when two or more are gathered in his name nothing is void. Could we pray right now together for this gift of meeting that God has given us?"

Basmah combed her fingers through Shaima's hair. She then lowered her head and grasped my hands. Together, as if the seas had never separated us, as if God was confirming our happenstance, we prayed.

# TO SEE IS TO SEEK

I walked back to my seat and to Jason. I felt a spirit of understanding as I buckled in for the landing. Jason took my hand as if he knew the whole time that God was working in a way that would soon be revealed.

The pilot had made good time. The flight was five hours and forty-five minutes from Dublin to Aleppo. As we descended, though, I felt a feeling of despair and heaviness came upon my heart. I prayed that God would lift it and show me the direction he intended for Jason and me to go.

We walked fast, as I wanted to catch up with Basmah. Her hijab covered her face. "Basmah, wait," I said loudly. She and Shaima were walking briskly through the airport. As I caught up with her, I noticed the people in the airport. Fighting between the government and rebel forces had devastated Aleppo, Syria's former economic capital. Looking into eyes of the people around me, I saw that devastation, the sadness, anger, and torture. "Basmah, here is the phone number where I am staying. It is the Al-Gawaher Hotel in central Aleppo. Please call me so I may visit with you and Shaima."

As we walked to baggage, a man approached her, and she made sure her hijab was over her face. She nodded to me. "Please don't forget," I said. With that, she picked up her one solitary baggage and, with Shaima in tow, left with the man.

"What was that all about? Did you give her our number at the hotel?" Jason inquired. I told him I did, but I felt a sense of foreboding of what was to come.

After we retrieved our bags, we tried to find a taxi, but couldn't. We had no choice but to find other means of transportation. It was a short jaunt to the hotel. The most common forms of transportation were taxis, rickshaws, or tuk-tuks, which were three wheelers. For short distances tuk-tuks are fine, but their small size made them uncomfortable for anything longer than thirty minutes. We had already been alerted to being charged higher prices for transportation, as the locals want to charge tourists higher fares. However, since it was a short ride to the hotel, we gave him four dollars in Syrian pounds and gave him the address to the hotel.

In the streets, one could see the devastation all around. What once stood as a beautiful museum, Aleppo National Museum, was now adorned with rubble, showing the struggle of the civil war.

As we checked into the hotel, I could feel all eyes on us. The bellboy helped us with our bags grudgingly. To relieve his distain, we tipped him two dollars in Syrian pounds. Then Jason went to his room, and mine was adjacent to his.

The hotel room was simple, with two beds and a table between them. It was clean, and the bathroom reminded me of my childhood. The balcony overlooked the city and the citadel in Aleppo.

In the lobby, people were sitting on couches, drinking coffee or tea and chatting with friends. It did not seem unfriendly, yet the air was thick with hatred for Americans. *What if ...?* I quickly dismissed the thought, fearing that what I was thinking was not what I came here to do.

Jason and I ordered Turkish coffee and looked at our itinerary, which was very limited. We came to Aleppo to go to the orphanage and see what we could find. What lay ahead of us needed prayer, so Jason and I knelt and prayed together. Jason was still not comfortable with praying out loud, so I did.

"Dear Lord, we have traveled so far, and while we do not know why you allowed us to come to the same conclusion, we do know that you are leading us. Put your angels in front, behind, and to the side of us as we seek the answers to our questions. Allow us to be humble in this foreign land. Let no enemy come between us as we find the solution. Allow us to be your servants as we seek your will on this journey. Amen."

# THE END OF LIFE AS THEY KNEW IT

The next morning proved uneventful in the hotel. Jason and I went down to breakfast. All around us, people looked at us questionably, at Jason more than myself. We ordered breakfast and were surprised to see how much food we received. Our breakfast consisted of Syrian cheese, which in America is known as string cheese, eggs, foul mdammas (fava beans salad), halawa, hummus, jams, laban Arabi (sheep's milk yogurt), laban baqari (cow's milk yogurt), labneh, makdous, olives (green and black), olive oil, qarisheh, shanklish, sliced cucumber, sliced tomato, za'tar, khubz Arabi (Arabic bread), and tea. I felt like I was in my grandmother's kitchen again. And Jason had no qualms in devouring our meal.

We didn't know where to go or who to ask, so we just took off on foot. We walked to the citadel, which is situated on a hill in the center of the city. It is visible from almost anywhere in Aleppo. Usage of the citadel hill dated back at least to the middle of the third millennium BC, but the current structure dated from the thirteenth century. It was considered to be one of the oldest and largest castles in the world. The citadel led into the old city of Aleppo. The devastation of war and its hatred was seen all around. Rebels encompassed it daily.

We walked farther into the old city of Aleppo. All around we could smell the aroma of the past along the market streets that are known as souqs. It took us back in time. Along the alleyways, we saw ottomans and savory dishes of food. There were merchants selling silk and other beautiful fabrics. Yet there was a feeling of heaviness all around. *Lord,* I thought, *this is your land, the land of the chosen. Why do you allow destruction to occur to your land, your people?* The evil was definite in the atmosphere of Aleppo.

My mind wandered. I thought of Basmah and Shaima. All I wanted to do was to hear from them.

We strolled through the streets of Aleppo, wanting confirmation of where to go. It was about 1:00 p.m. when we arrived back at the hotel.

There are two messages awaiting my arrival. One was from Kevin. I haven't even taken the time to call him in case someone might be listening to calls. I opened my computer and the Internet and quickly sent Kevin an e-mail telling him that we were all right, although tired and jetlagged, and that our next step was to go to the orphanage. I ended with telling him that I loved him and would call later at 9:00 p.m. Eastern time.

The second message was from Basmah. She had left a number for me to call. I quickly went to Jason's room. "Jason, Basmah wants us to call her. Maybe this is the answer we have been waiting for. What do you think?"

"Are you kidding? We came all this way, and you are asking me if you should call? Absolutely, Prof! Call! Don't take another step away from the phone. Call now. We are finally living the answer to our questions."

# Open Eyes Are the
# Roots of the Soul

I called Basmah. She sounded cheerful. *How could she be cheerful in the rubble of this city?* I thought.

"Ah, Michelle, so nice to hear from you. I wanted to invite you to come to the orphanage so you can find the answers you are looking for. Your questions will be answered. God has spoken to me."

I was ecstatic. God was answering questions. We just had to keep our eyes and hearts open.

Basmah gave me directions to the Aleppo orphanage. Jason and I flagged down a taxi in the heart of the city. Taxis were a little more expensive. We paid $20.00 SYP, but it was worth it.

The orphanage was about twenty miles outside the walls of Aleppo. The travel was arduous, as the road was bumpy. Yet our hearts were beating with excitement, for we knew soon we would have a clearer picture of God's will for this journey.

We arrived at the orphanage about forty-five minutes after we left the hotel. There was a small bridge over a stream of water. Funny how even here a bridge came to mind. The buildings were one-story simple construction and painted beige. Inside, the walls were painted white. We knocked on the aluminum door. A young slender Arab woman in a brown hijab opened the door. She greeted us, "As-salam alaykom."

No pictures were hung on the walls. Inside the main room, the bedrooms that housed ten cots to a room were modest. Thin bedding lined the thin mattresses. It wasn't as dirty as I had expected, nor was it as homey as my home. The floors were bare with only a small rug at the end of the rectangular room. The room was very crowded with twenty-five children to each sleeping room. Those children who did not have cots were given a thin pillow, barely enough for cushion, and a blanket.

I turned to Basmah. "Where are the children?"

"They are out in the playground for now. What with the fighting and all, we have to guard the children, but we also have to give them the freedom to play. Come with me so you can meet some of them."

As we walked into the courtyard, we met a small, slender girl. Her name was Malak . Basmah explained that Malak was a shy girl from the outskirts of Homs. Her father had been killed by the Syrian army recently. Basmah went on to say that it had been almost two years since Malak last went to school. The sadness in her eyes told the story all too well.

"As-salam alaykom, Malak," I said.

The young girl put a faint smile on her face. "As-salam alaykom," she replied. We then walked on to the other children gathered around one swing.

Basmah turned to us. "A child has the right to learn and to play, but so many have lost the rights of a home and a family."

Tears welled up in my eyes. This was what I had been called to do on this journey. Jason and I were sent here to do something. Children were caught up in a religious conflict they had been born into. My heart was silent with heaviness. How could this barbaric war claim the innocent as its victims?

We spotted Shaima in the middle of the group. She was laughing as they choose her to be "it" in a simple game of *hajla*.

A young girl came up to us. Her name was Nurmeen. She was a little rounder, fed well by the orphanage in comparison to the other children in the courtyard. Her parents came to Aleppo from the University in Damascus. However, on a day when they should have been enjoying going to the marketplace, her parents were gunned down amidst others.

Nurmeen explained to us in broken English that hajla is a playground game where a group of players toss an object, usually a stone, through patterns of squares outlined on the ground, hopping through spaces with one leg. "You draw four squares on the ground. Then you must push a small stone through the line, using one leg," she said. The trick, however, was to make sure the stone landed inside the square, not on the lines dividing them. "One wins the game if he or she does not make any mistakes. If all make mistakes, the game is restarted until a winner is declared. The rules of the game can be bent sometimes for children who have never played before, but," she smiled, "an even number of children have to play."

Thank you, Nurmeen, for explaining to us," Jason replied. As they were talking, my focus went to Shaima. She ran to me and hugged me so tight that I almost fell over.

"Shaima, you almost knocked me over!" I laughed a hearty laugh. The other children in the circle also start to laugh.

The sun was high upon us, and it was quite hot in the courtyard. Basmah motioned for the children to come inside for something to eat. Their snack included some zatoon (olives) and zata (pita bread with sesame), and they drank water from the pump outside. There were so many children without parents, without hope.

*Jason and I have sought and found, but now what, dear Lord? What do you want us to accomplish here?*

# A Call in the Night
# an Answer to Prayer

We arrived back at the hotel, exhausted but fulfilled. God had given us a glimpse of how these poor children were living daily. My heart ached for them. Jason also felt that he had received glimpses of his childhood through this.

I had to call Kevin. It had been almost two days since I had spoken with him. As I dialed a Skype connection, I couldn't help but wonder about Shaima. She was so beautiful and innocent and a smart little girl. More importantly, the reason she stood in my mind was that she reminded me of the little girl in my visions. What if God …? I focused my attention on the computer as Kevin appeared on the screen.

"Hi, gorgeous," he said. He looked weary. I bet he wasn't getting enough sleep.

"Hey, handsome. How are you?" I smiled, knowing without his even saying so that he missed me.

"It is not the same without you here. Life goes on while you are finding answers to your questions."

We spoke for the next half hour about the orphanage and Shaima. "Kevin, she just really has touched my heart. I feel such a connection to her. I can't explain it, but she looks so much like the little girl in my visions. What do you make of it?"

Kevin thought for a moment. "Why is she there? What happened to her family?" I explained to him all the details that I knew. "Michie, you are impulsive at times, but if you have sought God on this, there may be a connection after all." I loved the way he always understood me. He was my hero, the man who God had chosen for me. How I loved him!

# A Rainbow in the Clouds

By now, Jason and I were spending every day at the orphanage, helping Basmah and the other adults care for the children. But our time was coming to a close. I was so torn. I had spoken of Shaima many times to Jason. He came to the same conclusion that Kevin did, only neither was said so in a straightforward manner.

"Prof, you are a smart woman, someone I admire. I think you know what you have to do. Take her home to the United States. She belongs with a loving family. You and your mister are the family."

I thought about this at least one hundred times a day since meeting Basmah and Shaima. "Jason, while the kids are quiet, I think I am going for a walk on the bridge."

He smiled. He knew my heart almost as well as Kevin. "Sure thing, Prof. I am just going to help Basmah with the evening meal before we head back to the hotel."

I started to walk across to the bridge. It was cloudy. I became reverent, as I felt the presence of the Lord. I looked to the sky and closed my eyes. "Lord, is this what this journey was about? Was I to find Shaima and take her home as my little girl?"

I felt the Lord say, "Fear not, my child, I am with you always."

I was taken aback by the response. Audible or inaudible, it was clear. I was to have no fear in my—our—decision, Kevin's and mine. I knew the time had come.

I walked back across the bridge. I glanced up, and there before my eyes was a rainbow. God's promise. He will never leave us or forsake us. This confirmed my feelings even more.

It was midnight back in New York, but I didn't care. I had to tell Kevin what had just happened. I ran back to the orphanage with my feet almost off the ground!

I looked for Basmah and found her and Jason in the kitchen of the orphanage. "Basmah, would it, I mean, could I ..." I was not sure what exact words and feelings I wanted to convey.

"My dear Michie," Basmah said. "I know what you are going to ask me, and the answer is yes. You can adopt Shaima. There is a lot of red tape, but I know many couples who have adopted from our orphanage here in Aleppo. We just have to get the paperwork started."

I could do nothing but sit on the floor and cry. Here, now, my dream of being a mother was going to come true. Here, now, the Lord had blessed the decision. The little girl in my vision was not me but Shaima. The Lord had given me this vision so long ago for this exact journey to find her. I was about to end her sad yesterdays and begin her happy tomorrows with God's help. And everyone else's.

Basmah knelt down to me. "Michie, Shaima loves and adores you. Yes, there is the language barrier for now. But she has no one else. Her life here is tortuous only because she longs for a family. It is your journey to be her mother, God has promised that."

Jason knelt beside me and prayed, "Lord, you have brought us all around the world to come to this moment. We thank you for bringing us here to be your servants. Prof and her husband need Shaima. I needed to come to complete my mission. Now as we forge ahead, be our strength and our guide. Help us help Shaima walk into a new way of life. A life filled with friends and family, without fear of being killed or tortured. Help us to see the bridge that hugs tomorrow. You alone make miracles happen. We ask that you give us the freedom to do this."

Yes, there would be many obstacles ahead. I already knew that. But my heritage had brought me to this moment where I could give a little girl a tomorrow with no fears of yesterday. My job was completed. The bridge of events and countries, of culture and love, was built. Shaima would grow to love her Middle Eastern ways. She would grow up as I did, loving who she is and loving the bridges of her life. The connection of those bridges would be emblazoned on her heart. I would see to that. She would never forget who she was, her heritage, and how, by God's grace, I became her mom!

# THE BRIDGE TO HOME

Jason and I had many miles of red tape to complete in order to accomplish our tasks ahead: Jason's to come and be a missionary in Aleppo and mine to become a mother for Shaima. Kevin was ecstatic at the thought of fatherhood. I was certain that God had placed us here for this reason, to be the parents of Shaima, the little girl who was first just a vision in my dreams to now the reality of an angel standing beside me.

Basmah helped with the paperwork. We had to hire an experienced immigration lawyer. His name was James Bartholomew, a resident of Florida. His extensive experience and being a Christian helped the process along. I was so amazed at God's miracles. Before I even understood it, he had showed me the daughter of my dreams. The daughter who would be my legacy.

# Our Dream of
# a Miracle

The adoption would take about six weeks. I had to call Suzie and tell her. I also had to call the dean. I knew I was letting them down. But when miracles happen, there is always a way.

But my foresight proved to be wrong. They understood completely and were very happy for me. The only setback was that I couldn't see Kevin beforehand. He was ecstatic! A daughter he could call his own! It was a dream that neither one of us imagined would come true.

Kevin thought about coming to Aleppo. However, his position at work would not allow him to be away that long. We Skyped as often as we could, but it was hard to get service at the orphanage. Kevin, my prince, spoke with Shaima with so much love in his voice.

She didn't quite understand, but she understood that there were people who would love her for a lifetime. Shaima would never have to worry about being alone again. Basmah made sure that Shaima understood that.

Every time she saw me, Shaima ran and hugged me so tightly. My daughter! What an exhilarating … no, miraculous feeling it was! And when Shaima Skyped with Kevin, she lit up like an angel.

# The First of Many
# New Bridges

The day finally came for the adoption clearance. It seemed like it would never come. However, when it did, it took less than two hours. Shaima and I were ready to go home. Jason, on the other hand, had a different dream.

"Prof, I have decided that I am not going back to the United States. As you walked to the bridge that day, I saw my bridge. God showed me that I need to be here for as long as he lets me to help these children. They need a role model of what a man truly is. Not one who seeks to hurt, kill, and destroy, but one who will guide, love, and show them how to live. It was a tough decision, but I have come to a conclusion. My true job is to show them the bridge to a new way of life. Besides, I won't have to suffer in your class anymore!" Jason laughed, but I started to cry. He looked at me curiously. "Why all the tears? We can Skype. You can tell me about all the frustration of not getting through to your students, and I can tell you about the joys of serving those who need it the most."

We hugged. Not as a professor and student, but as two people who connected through the love of the Middle East. I understood now our connection. We both had the same goal. However, to an outsider it may have appeared different. I had found my diamond, and Jason had found his. He just had to polish all of them just a little bit more. Perhaps one day Jason would find his bride, but for now, the love of the orphanage and the children made him happy.

I would be sad not to have him nearby as a friend, a brother, but as he said, we could Skype.

# "Ah lah proh-shen fwah" or Until We Meet Again

Basmah helped pack Shaima's minimal belongings. She possessed a few outfits and, of course, her precious doll. Shaima seemed timid about the adventure, but she was happy. She had a new family. Kevin and I had a daughter, and our dream of a circle of love would be complete. Shaima would be introduced to all her cousins, aunts, and uncles and live a life free of hurt, fear, and insecurity. Our love would wrap around her like a blanket and protect her for the rest of her life. She would feel the same love I knew growing up, and Kevin would give her the love he had lost at such a young age.

The time came to say good-bye. Shaima cried when she hugged her friends. I am sure that she thought she would never see them again. Yet Jason was there and Basmah. I would make sure that she kept in touch with them, and Basmah reassured her that this would be the case. I hugged Basmah and told her that God's miracle came through because of her help.

I cried when saying good-bye to Jason. Then we all held hands and prayed a prayer of thanksgiving to God. We also prayed that the other children would find permanent safe havens where they would no longer feel fear but security as well as love. Until that time, Jason and Basmah would make sure they received both.

# HOME SWEET HOME

The trip home was arduous and long, but this time I had precious baggage with me. My daughter. How strange that sounded! Shaima was mine. There were still so many obstacles to clear. But one thing for certain was that I would no longer see the little girl under the lamppost, for she was now with me in the flesh. Shaima connected me to the past of my heritage and was a part of my present and future.

As we descended into New York, Shaima saw the Statue of Liberty. She was mesmerized. I tried to explain to her that this was given as a sign of friendship. Of course, I had to use mostly sign language of sorts, as her English and my Arabic were yet to be perfected. We were both students and teachers, each with something to give the other.

When I saw the Brooklyn Bridge, tears came to my eyes. All my life there has been a bridge. I never knew why there was such significance in bridges until this moment. This was my bridge. My connection. Shaima, my daughter, who I had waited for all my life, was the bridge of a dream, and the dream was now a reality. I didn't have to look for bridges of the past. God had seen to that. We now had all the connections we would ever need, Kevin and I.

I didn't know what the future would bring. But I did know that whatever came our way, we would handle it as a family with love, honor, and respect. Shaima would grow up to be a beautiful woman, never forgetting her roots, just as I have never forgotten mine.

We departed from the plane and went through customs. When asked by the customs agents, I simply told them that my daughter and I were coming home from a long journey. They smiled. God had made the impossible possible.

I then spotted Kevin. He held two bouquets: a big one of roses for me and a little one of roses for Shaima. As we turned the corner to greet him, he had tears in his eyes. It had been so long that I had almost forgotten how he could stand out in a crowd and be my sole attention.

I almost flew into his arms with Shaima in tow. I gave him a kiss, although not a lingering one, but I wanted to. I then bent down and so did Kevin. "Shaima, this is your baba. He loves you with all his heart."

Unexpectedly and miraculously, Shaima understood. She hugged him as if she would never let go. And the glow on his face was so touching and loving.

Finally, we were complete. God had seen to that. When Shaima was sad, we would comfort her. When she was sick, we would care for her. When she was insecure, we would reassure her. But most importantly, when she was happy, we would rejoice with her.

This was only the beginning of many memories. I didn't know what the future held for a family with many past memories. But I did know that we were starting right there in that moment making new memories to last a lifetime. And we owed it all to our Lord, Jesus Christ. Thank you, Jesus!

Kevin gathered our luggage, what little there was of it. Then with Shaima holding both our hands, Kevin said, "Let's go home. Home. What a wonderful word, a wonderful place."

# NOTES

1   Referring to the recent stabbing to death and throat slitting of Parvaneh Eskandari by her husband, Dariush Foruhar. Vida Hajebi. *Arash,* no. 69 (1999).

2   According to the justice ministry, the *dyeh* for a man is equivalent to $20,000 on the current exchange rate (or 100 camels or 200 cows or 1000 sheep). That of women is half.

3   See for example: Shirin Ebadi. "Women in Law in Iran" (*vazi'ate hoghughi zanan dar iran*). *Jameh Salem,* no. 27 (August 1996): 42–50.

4   The last two carry a death sentence.

5   See for example: Dr. Fatmah Ghaem Zadeh. "Violence against Women" (*badraftari ba zanan*). *Jameh Salem,* no. 28 (September 1996): 56–59.

6   Dr Karim Ezzati Zadeh. *Jameh Salem,* no. 28 (September 1996): 52–53.

# BIBLIOGRAPHY

"Proverbs 31-New International Version," Bible Gateway, accessed November 25, 2015, https://www.biblegateway.com/passage/?search=proverbs+31&version=NIV.

"Berlin's Suicide-Proof Nuclear Fallout Shelters," Vice Media, LLC, accessed March 7, 2013, http://www.vice.com/read/berlins-suicide-proof-nuclear-fallout-shelte..

Cloud, John. "Atta's Odyssey." Time. Time, 30 Sept. 2001. Web. 25 Nov. 2015.

Ezzat, Dr. Ahraf. "9/11 Hijacker Mohamed Atta & the Unreported Story." Veterans Today. Journal for the Clandestine Community, 10 Sept. 2010. Web. 25 Nov. 201

"False Pregnancy (Pseudocyesis)," WebMD, LLC, accessed November15,2015), http://www.webmd.com/baby/guide/false-pregnancy-pseudocyesis).

"Law metaphors Eslami Ba reforms and others" Alhaqat Ta shahrivar 390. (2013, April 4), accessed November 15, 2015, http://www.iranhrdc.org/persian/permalink/3310.html#.UVv6b5Ntgd0.

Sahebjam, F. *The Stoning of Soraya M.* New York: Arcade, 1994.

"Syrian Arab Republic," <u>Gender</u> Equality Inc. 2014. Accessed Web. 21 Nov. 2015. https://www.unric.org/en/unric-library/26585

Yong, William. "Iran Denies Freeing Condemned Woman." *New York Times,* December 10, 2010.

# Author Biography

After 9/11, Dr. Minerva Santerre felt she had to tell how much growing up in a Syrian household mattered and how her memories of cherished family time is still close to her heart today. Through this novel, Dr. Santerre interweaves her own childhood with that of the characters that come alive within the pages.

Dr. Santerre has taught gifted elementary classes for thirty years. She is also a professor at Miami-Dade Community College. She has worked closely with other organizations as a grant writer and curriculum developer. The love of the Lord has always given her the courage she needed. She lives in Miami, Florida, with her husband. Dr. Santerre has three grown sons, two daughter in loves and the diamonds of her life are her four grandchildren. Her mother is still living at 93 years old with her. When Dr. Santerre isn't teaching, her love of writing is inspired by her faith.

Printed in the United States
By Bookmasters